Enid Blyton
RAINY DAY STORIES

Look out for all of these enchanting story collections

by *Enid Blyton*

Enid Blyton

RAINY DAY STORIES

HODDER CHILDREN'S BOOKS

This collection first published in Great Britain in 2021
by Hodder & Stoughton

1 3 5 7 9 10 8 6 4 2

A CIP catalogue record for this book is available from the British Library.

ISBN 978 1 444 95636 8

Typeset by Avon DataSet Ltd, Arden Court, Alcester, Warwickshire

Printed and bound in Great Britain by Clays Ltd, Elcograf S.p.A.

The paper and board used in this book are made from
wood from responsible sources.

Hodder Children's Books
An imprint of Hachette Children's Group
Part of Hodder & Stoughton
Carmelite House
50 Victoria Embankment
London EC4Y 0DZ

An Hachette UK Company
www.hachette.co.uk
www.hachettechildrens.co.uk

Contents

Mrs Twiddle's Umbrella

Mrs Twiddle's Umbrella

'I'M JUST going out to fetch my paper,' Mr Twiddle called to Mrs Twiddle. 'I won't be long.'

'Take your umbrella then, because it's raining hard,' called back Mrs Twiddle.

Twiddle looked for his umbrella. He couldn't find it anywhere. It wasn't in the hallstand, it wasn't hanging up with his coat, it wasn't upstairs in his bedroom.

'That tiresome umbrella!' muttered Mr Twiddle to himself. 'It's always disappearing. Could I have left it anywhere, I wonder.'

He thought hard. He might have left it at the post office. He might have left it at the butcher's. He might have left it at the fishmonger's. There were any amount of places where he had already left it at one time or another and might have left it again the last time it rained.

Twiddle felt guilty. Mrs Twiddle always had a lot to say when he couldn't find his umbrella. She would make him go and ask at every shop in the town if she knew it wasn't in the hallstand.

'Haven't you gone yet?' called Mrs Twiddle. 'Do go, dear. I want you back in good time for dinner, you know. And bring back some fish for the cat, will you?'

'All right,' called Twiddle. 'Though I don't know why that cat should have so much fish. It has far more than we do. And I do hate carrying fish home on a wet day. It smells so, and—'

'Now, Twiddle, take a basket and go,' called Mrs Twiddle. 'Do you want me to come and button your coat and find your hat and put up your umbrella for you? Really, if I don't, you'll never get away this morning.'

Twiddle looked once more at the hallstand in

despair. Where, oh, where was his tiresome umbrella? He heard Mrs Twiddle coming, and he snatched at the only umbrella in the stand. It belonged to Mrs Twiddle. Never mind, he would borrow it just this once.

He rushed out of the front door and banged it behind him. He buttoned his coat and put up his umbrella as he went down the path, afraid that Mrs Twiddle might call him back. She would be very cross if she knew he couldn't find his own umbrella and had taken hers.

Mr Twiddle went to get his paper. He stuffed it into his pocket because he didn't want it to get wet. Then he actually remembered to call at the fish shop for some fish for the cat. Twiddle didn't like his wife's cat. It always sat just where he could fall over it.

The fishmonger stuffed some fish heads and fish tails into a bit of paper. Mr Twiddle took the parcel in disgust. Why hadn't he brought a basket as Mrs Twiddle had suggested? Now his hands would smell of fish all day.

He put up his umbrella again and walked off down the street. Somebody called to him. 'Hey, Mr Twiddle! The sun is out and the rain's stopped. Why have you got your umbrella up?'

Twiddle stopped at once, feeling very foolish. Yes, it was a lovely sunny morning now, and he hadn't noticed. He tried to put the umbrella down with one hand, because he had the fish in the other, but he couldn't. It was too stiff. So he put the fish on a wall for a moment and then managed to put the umbrella down.

'Meeow!' said a delighted voice, and a big tabby cat jumped up beside the fish. It tore at the bit of paper that wrapped it.

'Stop that!' said Twiddle crossly, and gave the cat a prod with his umbrella. It yowled and disappeared, taking with it the paper the fish had been wrapped in.

'Bother!' said Twiddle, annoyed. 'Now the fish hasn't got any paper – look at all the heads and tails slithering about on the wall. I can't carry them like that.'

6

He remembered his own newspaper safely stuffed in his pocket. He'd have to wrap the fish in that. How horrid! Still, there was nothing else to be done.

Twiddle carefully hooked his wife's umbrella on the branch of a tree that hung down over the wall. He wrapped the fish scraps in his paper, and walked off down the street.

He left his wife's umbrella behind him, of course. He never once thought of it until the rain suddenly began to fall again. Then he found he hadn't an umbrella to put up!

'Oh, my! I hooked it on to that branch by the wall where I wrapped up the fish in my paper,' he groaned, and rushed back to get it.

But it wasn't there. Not a sign of an umbrella could he see! He called out to the woman in the little sweet shop opposite.

'Did you see anyone take an umbrella from this branch here? I left it not long ago.'

'Oh, yes,' called back the sweet-shop woman.

'Somebody took it not five minutes ago.'

'The thief!' said Twiddle indignantly. 'What was he like?'

'It wasn't a he; it was a she,' said the woman. 'It was somebody dressed in a blue mackintosh and a hat with daisies on. She was rather plump, and hurried along like anything.'

'Thank you!' called Twiddle. 'I'll track down that nasty woman, if it takes me all morning!'

So off he went, hunting for a plump woman in a blue mackintosh and a hat with daisies on it. He couldn't see her anywhere. He stopped a man on a corner and asked him if he had seen anyone dressed like that.

'Yes,' said the man. 'She passed me at the bottom of that road. She was going towards the bicycle shop, if you know where that is.'

Twiddle did. He raced along to the bicycle shop, getting wetter and wetter as the rain poured down. He felt very angry indeed. To think that that thief of a woman should steal his wife's umbrella and send him on a goose chase like this in the pouring rain.

He went into the shop. 'Did somebody wearing a blue mackintosh and a hat with daisies on come in here?' he asked. 'Somebody with a very nice umbrella – with a dog's head on the crook handle?'

'Yes,' said the boy there. 'She did. She said she was going down to the baker's – you might get her there.'

Off went Twiddle to the baker's. He peered inside. Nobody there at all. 'What do you want?' called the baker's wife.

'Somebody in a blue mackintosh and a hat with daisies,' called Twiddle in despair.

'Oh, she came in for a cake just now,' said the woman. 'She's only just gone. Hurry round the corner and you'll catch her!'

Twiddle hurried – ah, there was somebody in a blue mackintosh and hat with daisies, scurrying along with an umbrella up – his wife's umbrella too!

How dared the woman be such a thief? She deserved to go to prison.

At that very moment Mr Plod, the policeman, came round a corner and nearly bumped into Twiddle.

'Morning, Mr Twiddle,' said Mr Plod. 'How wet you are! I thought only policemen had to go out in the rain without umbrellas!'

'Mr Plod, you're just the man I want,' said Mr Twiddle eagerly. 'Someone's stolen my wife's umbrella, and the thief is there – look, down the road in front of us – with the very umbrella! What shall I do?'

'I'll deal with this,' said Mr Plod. 'That's what policemen are for. Come along with me, sir.'

So Mr Plod and Mr Twiddle hurried after the thief in the blue mackintosh. Aha! She would soon be very frightened indeed.

'There – she's gone into Mrs Chatter's house,' said Mr Plod. 'We'll have to go and knock at the door and get in and face her. Come along.'

Mr Plod knocked loudly at the door. Mrs Chatter opened it and Mr Plod walked in.

Mr Twiddle stayed at the front door. He thought he would let Mr Plod deal with this. He heard the policeman's rumbling voice.

'I've had a report that an umbrella has been stolen,' he said. 'Was it you, madam, who took it?'

A voice answered him indignantly. 'Yes, it was me – and why shouldn't I take it? It was my own umbrella! There it was, hanging on the branch of a tree in the middle of the village street – my umbrella! I'd like to know who put it there! Just wait till I find out who took my umbrella and hung it on a tree in the village street!'

'Dear me,' said Mr Plod. 'Are you sure it was your own umbrella? What is your name, madam?'

'You know my name quite well – I'm Mrs Twiddle!' said the voice indignantly.

Well, Mr Twiddle could have told Mr Plod that, of course. He knew his wife's voice very well indeed.

He stood shivering at the front door, feeling very upset indeed.

'You wait till Mr Twiddle hears about this,' went on Mrs Twiddle. 'He went out this morning with his own umbrella – a little later I remembered I had to go out too. But I couldn't find my umbrella at all, so I put on my oldest hat and my mackintosh and out I went without one. And just *imagine* how astonished I was suddenly to see my very own umbrella hanging on a tree in the village street! I couldn't believe my eyes.'

'Very strange,' agreed the policeman, wondering what Mr Twiddle was going to say about all this.

'And now you come banging at my friend's door and tell me somebody says I've stolen my own umbrella!' went on Mrs Twiddle. 'I never heard anything like it. Show me the person who says I stole it, and I'll show you the thief – it must be he who took my umbrella and hung it on that tree! He must be mad. He must be—'

Twiddle didn't wait to hear any more. Feeling very

sick indeed, he stole off down the path. He hoped Mr Plod wouldn't give him away. If only he could get home before Mrs Twiddle discovered anything more!

Mr Plod didn't give him away. He apologised to Mrs Twiddle and went off in a hurry before she could ask him any awkward questions. Mrs Twiddle went home with her umbrella, very cross indeed.

Twiddle had got there first He had opened the front door and had fallen over the cat, who, as usual, loved to sit in the very middle of the dark hall.

The cat sniffed him. He smelt very pleasantly of fish. Twiddle felt about for the fish he had bought.

But he hadn't got it. He had left it on the wall when he had gone back to look for the umbrella!

'If you think I'm going back there to look for your fish, you're mistaken, cat,' he said. But then he remembered that this morning's paper was round the fish – and he wouldn't be able to read the news if he didn't get the fish!

He groaned and went to the front door again,

followed by the excited cat.

He peered out. It was pouring with rain. He stepped out valiantly into it – and bumped into Mrs Twiddle hurrying down the path with her umbrella up!

'Twiddle, you're not going out again, are you?' she cried. 'I've got such a lot to tell you. Why are you going out again?'

'I've forgotten the cat's fish,' said Twiddle desperately.

'Oh, never mind for once,' said Mrs Twiddle, anxious to tell Twiddle the story of her umbrella and Mr Plod.

'I must go and get it,' said Twiddle, and shook himself away from his wife.

'Oh, Twiddle, it's very kind of you, but the cat can go without this time!' cried Mrs Twiddle. 'Come back. Where's your umbrella?'

'I don't know,' said Twiddle in despair.

'But, Twiddle, you went out with your umbrella this morning – I saw you!' cried Mrs Twiddle. 'Oh,

Twiddle, have you lost it again? Did you come home without it? Here take mine.'

'No, no, NO!' shouted Twiddle, who felt that he could never touch his wife's umbrella again. 'I'd rather get soaked!'

And off went poor old Twiddle into the rain to get back the fish and his paper. But the tabby cat had been there before him, so he won't find either. Really, he is a most unlucky fellow, isn't he?

It's Going to Rain!

ONCE UPON a time, when the Weather-Man was going down a dusty country lane he fell over a stone. He was carrying a rain spell in a little pot and some of it spilt when he fell.

'Bother!' said the Weather-Man, sitting up and rubbing his knees. 'I've spoilt my spell. Now we shall have too little rain!'

'You spilt it on me, you spilt it on *me*!' cried a tiny voice crossly. 'It hurts! It smarts! I don't like it. Take it away!'

'Oh, dear!' said the Weather-Man in alarm, and looked to see if the spell had fallen on a pixie or elf.

But it hadn't. It had fallen on a small plant with scarlet flowers, tiny and starlike. It was the scarlet pimpernel.

'I'm so sorry,' said the Weather-Man and got out his handkerchief. He wiped the little plant, but it still made a great fuss.

'It's horrid! It stings! The rain spell is much too strong; I don't like it.'

'Shut up your little red flowers then,' said the Weather-Man. 'It won't sting so much if you do. I'm really very sorry, pimpernel.'

He picked up his jar. It was only half full now. Dear, dear, what a lot must have been spilt over the poor little pimpernel! No wonder it had stung.

'I shall be dreadfully afraid of the rain now,' said the pimpernel. 'I want an umbrella in case the rain comes. That horrid rain spell has made me frightened of a rainstorm.'

'Oh, don't be silly,' said the Weather-Man. 'Whoever heard of a plant wanting an umbrella? Of course I shan't get you one. Be sensible.'

He went on his way and left the little pimpernel staring crossly at the big golden sun above. 'I shall always close my petals now when I know that rain is coming,' it said to itself. 'Always. If I don't, that rain spell may set to work again when it rains, and sting and smart.'

Now the next morning, when the sky was as blue as forget-me-nots the pimpernel suddenly shut up all its scarlet flowers. They closed very tightly indeed. Pip and Twinkle, two pixies passing by, called to it in surprise.

'What's the matter? Why are you shutting? Is it your early closing day, pimpernel?'

'Don't be silly,' said the pimpernel, opening one small scarlet eye. 'I don't have early closing days. I'm shutting my flowers because I know it's going to rain. I've had a rain spell spilt on me. That's how I know.'

'Storyteller!' said Pip. 'There isn't a cloud in the sky.'

'Well, you take my advice and go home for your

umbrellas,' said the pimpernel. But the pixies laughed and went on their way. Will you believe it, in an hour's time the sky clouded over and big drops of rain fell, soaking Pip and Twinkle to the skin! How they wished they had taken the pimpernel's advice. They went to talk to it again the next day.

'Pimpernel! You are very clever. Will you come and live in the garden beside our little house, so that you can always tell us what the weather is going to be? Then we shall never get soaked again.'

'Yes. I'll come. Dig me up carefully, roots and all,' said the pimpernel, feeling rather proud to be asked to grow in a garden, for it was really only a wild flower, a tiny weed.

So Pip and Twinkle dug it up very carefully, took it home in their little wheelbarrow and planted it in their garden. They watered it, made a fuss of it and then went to get their tea.

'We must hurry because we have to go to a meeting at six,' said Pip. Before they went, they ran over to the pimpernel. Dear me, what was this? It was shutting up all its petals, though the sun was shining brightly.

'It's going to rain,' it told the pixies. 'It is, really. I can feel it coming. I shall always know when rain is about now!'

The pimpernel spoke the truth. It *does* always know when it's going to rain. Would you like to prove it? Very well then, dig up a little plant, put it into a flowerpot and keep it on your windowsill.

It will tell you truly whenever it is going to rain, so you will always know whether to take an umbrella or not. Strange, isn't it?

The Tale of
Chuckle and Pip

The Tale of Chuckle and Pip

CHUCKLE AND Pip were two small pixies with pointed ears, twinkling eyes and merry voices. They made sunshades, umbrellas and parachutes, and were really very clever.

They had a shop just outside the king's palace walls, and they made the prettiest frilly sunshades, the gayest umbrellas and the strongest parachutes that ever were seen. The tiny money spiders bought the parachutes and used them when they wanted to leave their homes and go somewhere else. They swung the parachute into the air, caught hold of it and away they floated on the wind.

The fairies bought the sunshades and the umbrellas – but trade was very bad at the moment. The sun had not really been strong enough for sunshades, the spiders were quite content to stay at home and there had been no rain for weeks.

'We haven't sold a single umbrella, sunshade or parachute for ages,' said Chuckle gloomily.

'I know!' said Pip. 'I really don't know what we are going to do about it. If only the sun would shine all day long, we could sell our stock of sunshades – or if only it would rain, we could sell our umbrellas!'

'There's a party at the palace tomorrow,' said Chuckle. 'That means that everyone will pass our shop. Just suppose it poured with rain, Pip, when everyone was going by in their best! What a lot of umbrellas we should sell!'

Pip sat and thought. Yes, if only it would rain! If only they could *make* it rain! An idea came into his head – a very naughty one. He laughed.

'Chuckle, I've got a plan!' he said. 'What about me

climbing that big tree by the palace gate – with two or three watering cans full of water!'

'Are you mad, Pip?' asked Chuckle, puzzled.

'No,' said Pip. 'Don't you see the idea, Chuckle? As people go by in their best party frocks I'll water them with my watering can – and they'll think it's raining and go off in a great hurry to buy an umbrella from *you*!'

'Oooooh! That *is* a fine idea!' said naughty Chuckle, and he laughed till he cried. 'Can't *I* be the one to sit in the tree and water people, Pip?'

'No,' said Pip firmly. 'It's *my* idea and I shall do the watering. We'll put the cans of water up in the tree tonight when no one is looking.'

'But how can we climb a tree with a can of water in our hand?' said Chuckle.

'We shan't,' said Pip. '*I* shall climb up the tree, and let down a rope. You will tie the watering can carefully to the rope and I will haul it up and put it safely on that big broad branch on the west side of the tree.'

'You *are* clever at ideas, Pip,' said Chuckle. 'I'm longing for tonight!'

Well, that night the two naughty pixies carried out their plan. Pip climbed the tree and let down the rope. Chuckle tied a full watering can on to it. Pip hauled it up and hid it safely. Then he let down the rope again. He hauled up two big watering cans, one small one, and three hot-water cans as well, which he said he could use to fill the watering cans with when they were empty. Naughty Pip!

They went to bed. The next day was cloudy with no sun. But the clouds were too high for rain. Pip chuckled when he thought of how he was going to make rainy weather for all the palace guests that afternoon!

Chuckle put out all his prettiest umbrellas. Pip climbed the tree at three o'clock and waited patiently for the first person to come along.

It was Dame Thump in her very best blue silk dress with the red bows. Just as she walked beneath the tree Pip tipped up one of his watering cans.

Pitter-patter, pitter-patter! The water splashed down on Dame Thump. What a state she was in!

'Oh, my best frock! Oh, it will be spoilt before I get to the palace! Now who would have thought it would rain like this? If only I had an umbrella!' she said. Then she remembered that Chuckle's shop was nearby, and she hurried to buy a blue umbrella to match her frock. Chuckle was delighted.

Pip laughed so much that he nearly fell out of the tree. He just managed to save himself in time to give Dame Thump a gentle splashing as she passed by with her new umbrella held over her head.

Then came Mr and Mrs Spink with all their four children. They were very smart indeed. Mr Spink had on a yellow silk suit with hat and feather to match. Mrs Spink had on a frock as bright as the sun. All the children were dressed alike in red frocks and tunics.

Pip grinned. He tipped up his watering can. First he watered Mr Spink and his yellow hat. Then he watered Mrs Spink and her glittering frock.

Then he watered all the little Spinks, who cried out in dismay.

'Mother! Father! It's raining on our new dresses! Didn't you bring an umbrella?'

'No,' said Mr Spink, looking up at the sky. 'Dear, dear! Well, I think it's stopping now. Let's stand under this tree, dears, and we shall keep dry.' But it was no place to stand if they wanted to keep dry! Pip nearly burst himself with trying not to laugh, and he at once emptied a whole canful over the Spink family!

'Oh, the rain is simply pouring down!' said poor Mrs Spink. 'It's even soaking through the tree. Look! There is an umbrella shop, Mr Spink. We must certainly buy umbrellas, or we shall be soaked through before we arrive, and we don't want the dear king to think we are a family of drowned rats!'

They hurried to Chuckle's shop. They bought one big umbrella to share between Mr and Mrs Spink, and four tiny umbrellas, one for each child. Then they set off happily to the palace, holding them over their heads.

Pip laughed loudly, and Chuckle poked his head out of the shop door and laughed too. Then he caught sight of two or three more people coming along. 'Sh!' he said. 'Here are Fairy Trip, Pixie Tiptoe and Brownie Longbeard.'

Well, as soon as they passed under Pip's tree, Trip, Tiptoe and Longbeard got a good watering. How disgusted they were!

'Raining!' said Longbeard, shaking the drops out of his beautiful silvery beard. 'What bad luck!'

'And I left my umbrella at home!' said Fairy Trip.

'I shall be soaked!' said Tiptoe, who had on a very thin dress of spider's thread.

'What shall we do?' said Longbeard.

Pip helped them to think by watering them again.

They caught sight of Chuckle's shop. 'Look! He sells umbrellas!' they cried. 'Let's get some! We'll be all right then!'

Off they went and bought three expensive umbrellas. Then they set off to the palace once more, rather puzzled because the rain seemed to have completely stopped!

Pip was having a glorious time. He could hardly sit still in his hiding place he was so excited. To think that his idea was going so well!

Other guests came along and Pip watered them all. As everyone was in their best clothes they all rushed to get umbrellas. Soon Chuckle hadn't a single umbrella left and he began to sell his sunshades as umbrellas. He was doing very well indeed, though his customers were rather puzzled by his giggles! But as his name was Chuckle they thought he couldn't help giggling a bit.

Now when everyone arrived at the palace, complete with umbrellas, complaining of the rain, the king was most astonished.

'Raining!' he said. 'Impossible!'

'Not at all impossible, Your Majesty!' said

Longbeard. 'Look at my beard. It's soaked!'

'But I made a special bit of magic today to keep the rain off,' said the king. 'It can't possibly rain today.'

'Well, Your Majesty, it *did*,' said Fairy Trip. 'Just as we came to the gate it poured down!'

'Yes – by that big tree,' said Mr Spink. 'We had to go and buy umbrellas.'

'It was raining as *we* passed under that tree too,' said someone else.

'And it started just as I got there too,' said Dame Thump. 'But it didn't seem to be raining anywhere else.'

The king looked more and more surprised. 'Well,' he said, 'this is astonishing. First of all, I say that it could *not* rain today, because I made a spell against rain. And then you say that it only rained under that tree – when, as everyone knows, it rains all around if it rains at all, not just in one small place! This is puzzling! I must enquire into it!'

The king sent the Lord High Chamberlain down to

see into the matter. The chamberlain, who was a very rich and grand man, most beautifully dressed in cloth of gold, stepped down the palace drive to the gate. Then he walked haughtily to the big tree that stood by the gate.

Pip was still there. He saw the Lord High Chamberlain and grinned. My goodness, *if* only he could make *him* buy an umbrella or a sunshade, he would buy the finest one in the whole shop!

He tipped up a watering can – pitter-patter, down went the water! The chamberlain was most astonished and annoyed. Could it be raining after all? He looked up at the tree.

And he saw Pip's naughty, cheeky face peeping there! He knew at once what had been happening. He commanded the frightened pixie to come down and he fetched Chuckle too. Holding them by their big pointed ears, he took them back to the palace with him.

'These pixies watered everyone who passed by, so

that they would go and buy umbrellas,' said the Lord High Chamberlain in an awful voice.

'Is that so?' said the king, also in a very stern voice. 'Then I make a law in future that nobody in the whole of Fairyland shall buy anything from these two bad pixies. You may go, pixies.'

They went, crying bitterly. They knew that they would have hard work to make a living now, for nobody would buy from them. Poor Pip and Chuckle!

But they soon found a job with the dandelions, who were very good to them. Do you know what they do? Guess! Yes – they make those beautiful little parachutes that are fitted to every dandelion seed! Find a dandelion clock and take the seeds into your hand. You will see that you have dozens of little parachutes there, made of the finest hair. Blow them into the air and see how well they fly!

The Little Sugar Mouse

The Little Sugar Mouse

ONCE THERE was a little sugar mouse. He was made of pink sugar, and he had two eyes, two ears and a long string tail. He belonged to Elaine, and she wouldn't eat him.

'He's rather a dear,' she said to her mother. 'I like the way he looks at me. I shan't eat him, Mummy. He's quite the nicest mouse I've ever seen.'

Goodness! How grand the sugar mouse felt when he heard that. He sat on the window seat with the other toys, looking as important as he could. He was the nicest sugar mouse ever seen, he kept thinking to himself. Fancy that!

The other toys thought he was a funny little mouse. The big doll wanted him for a pet. The monkey wanted to cuddle him. The teddy bear wanted to stroke him. But the sugar mouse was vain and haughty. He thought himself very grand and important. So he was rude when they were nice to him.

'Leave me alone,' he said to the bear when the bear tried to stroke him. 'I'm not a dog!'

'Please don't try to cuddle me,' he said to the monkey when he wanted to pick the sugar mouse up. 'I'm not a baby. Go to the doll's house and get a doll from there if you want something to cuddle.'

'I will certainly not be a pet,' he said to the big doll when she wanted to take him on her knee. 'I am a grand and most important mouse – the nicest mouse Elaine has ever seen, she says!'

The toys grew tired of the sugar mouse's high-and-mighty ways. They wouldn't talk to him any more. Then he was cross because he wanted to talk to them, and kept telling them what a wonderful little mouse he was. He wanted them to say so too. So when they wouldn't talk to him he became very naughty and mischievous. He waited until the teddy bear was rather near the edge of the window seat, and then he ran at him with his sharp little sugar nose. He pushed the bear – and Teddy slid to the floor below with a bump. He was too big to climb up again by himself, and it made him very cross to hear the sugar mouse giggling away to himself above.

The sugar mouse annoyed the big doll too. He waited till she was asleep, with her eyes tight shut, and then he undid her shoelaces and all the buttons on her dress. She was really very puzzled.

'Every time I go to sleep my shoelaces and buttons are done up properly,' she said, 'and every time I wake they are all undone. Sugar mouse, if it is you playing this trick, I shall be very cross.'

But the sugar mouse played the worst trick of all on the monkey. Monkey had hair all over his body, and he was very proud of it because it was so thick, especially on his head. Well, the sugar mouse saw the tin of flour on the windowsill, where Mother had put it for a moment. And he climbed up to the tin, picked up a whole heap of white flour in his sugar paws, and threw it down on the monkey's head. In a second the monkey had white hair.

The toys stared at him in horror.

'Monkey! Have you suddenly grown old?' said the bear. 'Your hair is all white, as if you were an old, old monkey.'

The sugar mouse gave a giggle and nearly fell into the flour tin. The toys looked up.

'Oh! It's that tiresome sugar mouse again!' cried the monkey. 'Wait till I catch him! I'll bury him in the flour!'

But the sugar mouse was too quick for him. He hid in the brick box and wouldn't come out again till the toys were good-tempered again.

Then the toys made up their minds that they simply could not let the sugar mouse go anywhere with them.

Sometimes they all went for a walk round the playroom at night, and the mouse loved to trot along behind, looking at everything they passed – the big coal scuttle, the dancing fire, the doll's house in the corner and the enormous rocking horse.

Sometimes the toys even went into the garden – and that was a very great treat. Often they went out of the playroom door if it had been left open, and walked down the passage to peep into the big kitchen.

And now the sugar mouse was not allowed to go with them at all. The toys slipped off when he was asleep. He was very angry indeed. He made up his mind that he would go with them the very next time.

Well, the next time they went it was raining. The toys badly wanted to go into the garden because the big doll had a little umbrella, and both the teddy and the monkey had mackintoshes and sou'westers of their own. Elaine had bought them for them at the toyshop, and they had never worn them in the rain.

'I'm coming too,' said the sugar mouse when he saw

them putting on their rain things.

'You are not,' said the big doll. 'It's raining. Don't be silly. Sugar mice never go out in the wet.'

'Well, I shall,' said the sugar mouse. 'Anyway, why shouldn't sugar mice go out in the wet, if you do? You are just making that up.'

'No, I'm not,' said the big doll. 'I've always heard it said that sugar mice never go out in the wet, but I don't really know why that is. Anyway, don't be silly, sugar mouse – we don't want you with us, and it's dangerous for you to go out in the wet. I'm sure it is.'

'Well, I'm coming,' said the sugar mouse, and he ran along behind the doll with her umbrella, and the teddy and the monkey in their mackintoshes and sou'westers. They tried to make him go back, but he wouldn't. He was really very naughty. He poked the big doll, and he trod in a puddle and splashed the teddy from head to foot. They were very cross with him.

It was raining hard when they got into the garden. The doll didn't mind because she had her umbrella. The teddy and the monkey were as dry as could be, and very proud indeed of their mackintoshes. The bear's sou'wester kept falling down over his nose, so that he couldn't see, but he didn't really mind that. The raindrops fell, plop, plop, plop, on to the sugar mouse, who had no umbrella, no mackintosh and no sou'wester. At first he thought he didn't like it very much. He began to squeak. The toys turned round and stared at him.

'What is wrong with the sugar mouse?' asked the big doll in alarm. 'He's going small.'

'His eyes don't look at me any more,' said the monkey.

'His sugar paws have gone,' said the bear.

'Oh, please, I don't feel at all well,' said the sugar mouse in a little frightened voice. 'Comfort me, big doll. Cuddle me, monkey. Stroke me, bear. Be kind to me, please.'

47

Well, the toys were kind-hearted, so they went to pick up the sugar mouse and comfort him. But they couldn't pick him up. He was getting smaller – and smaller – and smaller!

And very soon he was gone altogether. The toys stared in dismay.

'Where has he gone?' said the big doll. 'We must take him home quickly. Where has he gone?'

'Sugar mouse, where have you gone?' cried the bear.

But there was no answer. There never would be. The silly, vain, mischievous little sugar mouse had melted in the rain! What a pity!

Only his tail was left. The big doll carried it sadly back to the playroom and put it on the window seat. There Elaine found it the next day – but no sugar mouse was there with the little tail.

'Somebody's eaten him!' cried Elaine, almost in tears. 'Oh, who ate my dear little sugar mouse?'

'The rain ate him,' said the big doll in a whisper. 'The rain ate him, Elaine. Oh, what a pity!'

Mr Binkle's Boots

Mr Binkle's Boots

MR BINKLE was a fat brownie who lived in the corner cottage in the village of Fuff. He was fat because he ate such a lot, and he ate such a lot because he was rich and could buy plenty of food.

But although he was rich, he was a mean, stingy fellow who never gave a penny away, and wouldn't dream of putting down a saucer of milk for a stray cat. If a beggar came to the door, he slammed it in his face and let his dog loose. He was not a very kind brownie, and the people in the village of Fuff didn't like him at all.

Mr Binkle was very friendly with His Highness,

Prince Mighty, who lived in Twinkling Palace on the hill beyond the village. Prince Mighty liked Mr Binkle because he flattered him so much.

'You are the handsomest prince in the world, Your Highness!' Mr Binkle would say. 'You are the most powerful prince and the greatest ruler!'

This was all nonsense, because Prince Mighty was an ugly little fellow, and as for being powerful, well, he couldn't even manage his own servants. He had no kingdom to rule over except for his palace grounds, and even they were not very big!

But he believed everything that Mr Binkle said and liked to have him to tea to hear all the nice things that the artful brownie was ready to tell him.

Mr Binkle was very proud of his friendship with Prince Mighty, and he wouldn't be friends with anyone else in Fuff. Not that anyone cared, for everybody thought he was a horrible little man, and laughed at him behind his back. Mr Binkle always looked down his nose when he met anyone in the village, and wouldn't even say good morning. So nobody said good morning to him.

One day Prince Mighty asked Mr Binkle to go to lunch with him at one o'clock. This was the first time he had been asked to lunch and the brownie was most excited.

I must have a new suit! he thought. *I must have a new hat! I must have new shoes!*

He went to the pixie tailor, and to the gnome shoemaker. He ordered a wonderful suit of yellow silk with gold buttons down the front and a blue satin cloak to go over his shoulders. He ordered a pair of blue shoes with long, pointed toes, and then he went to the pixie hatter's and bought a marvellous hat. It was yellow and had seven little points with bells on each. It made a lovely ringing noise, and Mr Binkle was thoroughly delighted with it.

'How smart I shall be!' he said to himself when all the things he ordered had been sent home. He laid them out on the bed and looked at them.

Prince Mighty will be quite jealous of me! he thought. *Ha, ha! What a fine village street with everyone staring at my fine new suit of clothes!*

When the great day came Mr Binkle had a big disappointment. The rain was pouring down, and the streets were running with water. There was mud everywhere, and Mr Binkle looked at his new shoes in dismay. They were not meant for walking through mud.

'Perhaps it will clear up before it is time to go,' he said, and he stood at the window to watch.

Presently the rain stopped and the sun came out. 'Hurrah!' said Mr Binkle. 'I shall be all right now! Except for my shoes, of course – now what can I do about them? I really can't walk through the muddy fields in these beautiful new shoes. I must put them safely in a bag and wear my boots.'

But when he went to get his boots he found that one of them had a large hole underneath that let the water in. Mr Binkle always caught a cold when his feet got wet and he didn't know what to do. And just as he was wondering there came a knock at the door.

'The baker,' said Mr Binkle to himself, and went to see. But it wasn't the baker. It was an old lady, dressed in a raggedy shawl and a pointed hat. She was holding up her yellow skirt out of the wet, and on her feet she wore a fine pair of high rubber boots.

'Good morning,' she said politely. 'Could you give me a crust of bread? I haven't had anything to eat since yesterday.'

'I don't like beggars,' said Mr Binkle crossly. 'Go away! I shan't give you anything at all.'

'Just a drink of water then,' said the old woman. 'That won't cost you anything.'

'No,' said Mr Binkle in his meanest voice. 'I pump my own water and I don't give it away to beggars. Go away!'

The old woman hitched up her skirts and walked down the garden path, mumbling to herself. As she went Mr Binkle caught sight of her rubber boots, and an idea came to him.

'Hey!' he called. 'Come back! Come back!'

The old woman came back, and stood at the door again.

'I'll buy those boots from you,' said Mr Binkle, pointing to them. 'I'll give you a piece of chicken pie and a drink of milk.'

'No,' said the old dame. 'They cost a lot of money. You give me some money and then you shall have them.'

'How much money?' asked Mr Binkle.

'Ten silver coins,' said the old woman.

Mr Binkle laughed loudly although he knew that they would be cheap for only ten silver coins.

'Fiddlesticks!' he said. 'What nonsense! Why, they're not even worth five! And I don't expect they would fit me anyhow.'

The old dame was hungry and she wanted something to eat. So she slipped off her boots and told Mr Binkle to try them. They fitted him perfectly! He meant to have them, and he wondered how he could get them for very little money.

'I'll get you the chicken pie and the milk,' he said, 'and you shall have my old boots to go off in instead of walking barefoot. And I'll give you a silver coin into the bargain!'

'No,' said the old dame crossly. 'That's not enough. Give me nine silver coins, the pie and your old boots. Then you shall have my nice new ones.'

'What, do you dare to argue with me?' cried Mr Binkle, pretending to be angry. 'I'll set the dog on you!'

The old woman looked at him. It was a strange look and Mr Binkle felt a shiver go down his back. Suppose the old dame was a witch? Then he laughed scornfully and went to his larder. He picked up half a chicken pie and a small bottle of milk, and went into the hall. He told the woman to put on his boots and he gave her one silver coin.

'Here you are,' he said. 'Now be off with you! I've treated you very well.'

'I tell you I want my boots back,' said the old woman angrily. 'I don't want this pie and only one silver coin. And as for these old boots of yours they're not even worth a penny, for they let the water in at the bottom.'

Mr Binkle pushed her out of the door, and then he pointed to the kennel where Snarly, his dog, lived. 'Go away quickly,' he said, 'or I will set Snarly free.'

The old woman was afraid of dogs, and mumbling and grumbling she ran down the garden path in Mr Binkle's old boots. When she got to the gate she looked back with a very strange sparkle in her eyes. She muttered a few words in a low voice and then went down the street. Ah, Mr Binkle, what magic words those were that you didn't hear!

Mr Binkle was delighted with himself and the rubber boots. Now he could go through the fields safely, and take his new shoes with him in a bag. He could change into them at the palace and arrive in Prince Mighty's dining room looking just as smart as smart could be!

He dressed himself in his yellow tunic, his blue cloak and his seven-pointed hat with the bells ringing merrily, and put his blue shoes in a bag.

Then he started off for the palace, singing a happy little song, and hoping that everybody in Fuff village would see him as he passed by.

But what a funny thing! When he got to the gate of his cottage the rubber boots suddenly became very tight, for all the world as if they were holding his feet and not meaning to let him go. And then they started to play tricks on Mr Binkle!

First they walked his feet to an extra large puddle and jumped right in! Splash! The water soaked his tunic and splashed his fine cloak. Mr Binkle was horrified. Whatever was happening? He hadn't meant to walk into the puddle and yet he had gone there. What a very peculiar thing!

Soon the boots walked him to a ditch full of black mud. They jumped into it, and of course poor Mr

Binkle had to go too! Splitter-splutter-splash! Black mud flew into the air and a large drop went into Mr Binkle's eye. Another drop ran down his fat nose and made him look very comical. As for his poor cloak, it was running with black mud!

'Good gracious me, what a terrible thing this is,' said Mr Binkle, almost crying. 'These boots must be bewitched. I must take them off before they do any more damage.'

He sat down on a post and tried to pull them off, but he couldn't. They held tightly to his feet, and no matter how he pulled they wouldn't budge an inch. At last he gave it up, and looked sadly at his spoilt tunic.

'I must go home,' he said. 'I shall have to change into my other clothes, for these are quite spoilt. I don't know what the prince would say if I went to lunch with him wearing these muddy things.'

He got up to go back to his cottage – but the boots had quite other ideas. No, they wanted to go somewhere else, and to Mr Binkle's horror they walked up the path in Mrs Dibble-Dabble's backyard and went right to her big dog's kennel. The dog growled and showed his teeth. Mr Binkle wanted to run away but he couldn't. Oh, my, what a dreadful thing it was!

The dog suddenly growled again, and one of the boots tapped him on the nose. The dog rushed at Mr Binkle and bit a piece out of his blue cloak. Then he growled at the mischievous boots, and they decided it was time to go away. Down the path they went, and Mrs Dibble-Dabble looked out of the window and shouted, 'It serves you right, Mr Binkle, for teasing my dog!'

He hadn't a moment to explain, for the boots ran him down the road to where a big tabby cat was lying asleep on a warm patch of sand. The boots trod on her tail, and the cat woke up with a hiss, flew at Mr Binkle and scratched his right hand. Then it tore a hole in his tunic, and Mr Binkle could have cried with dismay.

'You hateful boots!' he said. 'You hateful boots! If only I could take you off, I'd throw you into the nearest pool!'

The boots were having the time of their life! The old dame had put a spell on them and they were enjoying their pranks tremendously. What would they do next?

Aha! Look, there was Mr Ding-Dong the gnome sitting asleep on the seat in front of his house. His feet were stretched out in front of him, and the boots thought it would be great fun to tread on them. Mr Binkle guessed what they were going to do when he felt them taking him towards Ding-Dong, and he was afraid. Ding-Dong was a bad-tempered gnome, and there was no knowing what he might do.

The boots cared nothing for Mr Binkle's fears. They ran up to Ding-Dong and trod hard on his outstretched feet.

'Ooh!' Ding-Dong the gnome woke up with a shout. When he saw that it was Mr Binkle who had trodden on his toes he was very angry indeed. Mr Binkle gave a howl and tried to run away, but the boots held him there.

'I didn't mean any harm. These boots of mine are bewitched, and made me tread on your toes.'

'What a silly story!' said Ding-Dong scornfully. 'Be off with you.'

Fortunately the boots decided that they would go on their way again, so off they started. To Mr Binkle's dismay they took the path that led to the palace of Prince Mighty. Surely they were not going to take him there? Why, he was in a dreadful state and the prince would be disgusted with him.

Yes, sure enough, the boots were going to the palace, but on the way there they walked into every ditch, puddle and pond they came across, and poor Mr Binkle became muddier and wetter and more ragged with every step.

At last the boots walked him through the palace gate. The guard tried to stop Mr Binkle, but it was no use, the boots took him on. In through the palace door he walked, and, dear me, right into the prince's dining room! It was half past one, and the prince was looking as black as thunder, for Mr Binkle was half an hour late. He was eating his lunch alone when the brownie came into the room, leaving great black footprints behind him wherever he went.

The prince jumped up angrily and demanded to know who Mr Binkle was, for he did not recognise the brownie in his muddy state, his face dirty and his hair wet.

'I'm Binkle,' said the brownie, almost crying.

'BINKLE!' said the prince in amazement and anger. 'How dare you come here in this state! Why, you look like a chimney sweep – and half an hour late too! How dare you, I say!'

Mr Binkle was just going to explain that it was all the fault of the boots when they started dancing. Oh, dear me, how they kicked into the air and tap-tapped on the floor, making Mr Binkle so out of breath that he couldn't say a word, because of course he had to dance too! Prince Mighty watched him in the greatest astonishment, growing more and more angry.

'Stop!' he said. 'Stop! This is a rude and unseemly thing to do! You arrive here late and in a dirty suit, and instead of saying you are sorry you start to dance all over my new carpet in your horrible boots!'

The boots were cross to hear themselves called horrible, and they danced up to Prince Mighty and trod on his toes. Then they kicked him hard, though Mr Binkle tried his very hardest to stop them.

'BINKLE!' roared the prince in the biggest, angriest voice he had. 'How dare you! I'll have you locked up in a dungeon! Are you mad?'

The boots really were enjoying themselves. They suddenly jumped up on the table and began to dance among the dishes, and whenever they came to a saltcellar, mustard pot, rolls of bread or napkin rings they kicked them right off the table! Mr Binkle was simply horrified, but he had to go up on the table with the boots, and it looked for all the world as if it were he who was doing all these wicked things.

Prince Mighty rolled up his sleeves and ran at Mr Binkle. He pushed him right in the middle of the chest and the brownie was flung off the table and landed in a corner.

'Ooh! Don't!' he cried, the tears running down his cheeks. 'I tell you it's the boots that are doing all this, not me!'

But Prince Mighty just didn't believe him.

'Boots, is it?' he said scornfully. 'But whose legs are inside the boots, making them dance and kick, that's what I'd like to know! Boots indeed!'

He came up to Mr Binkle to push him again, and he looked so fierce that even the boots were frightened.

They jumped Mr Binkle to his feet and began to run away. They could run very fast indeed, and they were soon out of the palace and running down the steps with poor Mr Binkle panting loudly. The prince saw that he couldn't catch him, so, taking a handful of squashy tomatoes off the dining table, he hurled them with all his might at the unhappy brownie.

Splosh! Splosh! They hit Mr Binkle at the back of the neck, and burst all over his cloak. The boots hurried along, and not until they were well out of reach of the prince and his guards did they go more slowly.

But by now the magic was wearing out, and not much was left. They took Mr Binkle right through the village of Fuff, and he was terribly ashamed when everyone came out to look at him.

'Ho! Look at old Mr Binkle!' cried all the people in delighted surprise. 'Isn't he a sight? Ha, ha! Ho, ho!'

Mr Binkle blushed red, and wished the boots would hurry along – but the magic was almost gone, and the boots went very slowly indeed, quite tired out. At last they reached the corner cottage where the brownie lived, and walked slowly up the path. Mr Binkle sat down in the hall and looked at them. They were no longer holding his feet tightly, and he wondered if he could take them off.

He tried. They came off quite easily, and he heard them sigh when he tossed them into a corner. They could do no more mischief. The magic had all gone.

Mr Binkle sighed too. He took off his dirty, wet clothes and turned the water on to have a bath. Then he got into the hot water and lay down to soak off all the mud. And he began to think hard.

Prince Mighty will never be friends with me again, he thought. *And the people of Fuff will laugh whenever they see me, especially when they hear all that the boots made me do. They will say that the old dame did right to put a spell on the boots, because I was so mean to her.*

'Well,' said Mr Binkle honestly to himself, 'I was mean. When I think about myself, I see that I am a proud, stuck-up, mean, stingy fellow. Nobody likes me, and I've a good mind to pack up my things and go where nobody knows me.

'But, no – I won't. That wouldn't be at all a brave thing to do. I shall stay here, and if people point their fingers at me and laugh, I will say, "Yes, laugh at me. I deserve it." I shall stay here and try to be different.'

He did stay, and he did try. Of course everyone pointed their fingers at him, and Prince Mighty never asked him to lunch again, but Mr Binkle tried not to mind. He gave pennies to the children, and bones to hungry dogs, and saucers of milk to stray cats – and when next he saw the old dame he gave her back her boots and ten silver coins as well. She was surprised!

And now Mr Binkle is very happy, because the people of Fuff village like him, and make quite a fuss of him. But if ever he gets a little bit pleased with himself, he frowns and says, 'Mr Binkle, be careful. Remember those boots!'

The Tale of Scissors the Gnome

The Tale of Scissors
the Gnome

THERE WAS once a tiny old man called Scissors. He was a gnome, and if you measure out three inches on your ruler, and cut out a little man that high, you will know just how small Scissors was!

He carried a pair of scissors about half as high as himself, and with them he cut out anything his friends wanted. A snip of his scissors and a coat would be cut out. Another snip or two and a party frock would be all ready for sewing up. He was a wonder with his scissors was the old gnome.

There was just one thing he was afraid of and that was rather strange, for he was afraid of the rain. We love to feel the rain on our faces, but Scissors was terrified. One big drop of rain on his head and he would be knocked flat on the ground, for he was so small. Once a drop of rain had broken his arm and he hadn't been able to cut out clothes with his scissors for three months.

Raindrops were as big as dinner plates to him! So you can guess that if it began to rain, Scissors would run for shelter at once. If ever he went out he took with him his green umbrella, which was four inches round and covered him well.

And then one day, when he had gone to visit the elf in the garden bed, somebody stole his umbrella. He had put it down for one moment while he cut out a pink dress and somebody crept up behind him and ran off with his precious umbrella!

Poor Scissors! No sooner did he miss his green umbrella than it began to rain! Plop! A drop fell on his head and sent him on his nose. Plop! One went on his back and took away all his breath. Plop! A third drop made him so wet that he looked as if he had been swimming for weeks.

'Help! Help! Lend me an umbrella, please!' yelled Scissors. But nobody was near except the elf whose dress he had been making. She was a scatterbrained little creature and didn't know what to do.

But nearby was a strong nasturtium plant, and the flowers called to Scissors. 'Pick one of our flat leaves! They will shelter you well. They are just like flat umbrellas!'

So Scissors gratefully picked a leaf, held it by the stalk and stood under it while the rain poured down. It made a wonderful umbrella, and Scissors was pleased.

'I'd like to do something for you, nasturtiums,' he said, when the rainstorm was over. 'What can I do? Do you want any dresses, coats or hats cut out to wear?'

'Of course not!' laughed the nasturtiums. 'We already have orange and yellow dresses to wear. But you might cut us a pretty little fringe in the centre, Scissors – a nice whiskery one.'

So the gnome took his scissors and cut a fine fringe in the middle of the flowers. And if you don't believe me, go and look! As for his umbrella, Scissors never found it, but he always keeps a stock of nasturtium umbrellas in water, ready for when he goes out. Isn't he funny and wise too!

This is My Place!

This is My Place!

ONE DAY a tiny seed fell down among the grass roots on a lawn. It lay there for a while, and then a drop of rain trickled down to it – one drop out of a passing shower.

The little seed liked it. It swelled up a little and waited for another drop of rain to come.

Later that week a heavy storm came and the rain pelted down in long slanting lines. The ponds were filled to the brim. Puddles shone down all the lanes. Roofs of houses were wet and shiny.

The little seed had all the water it needed, as raindrop after raindrop trickled down into the earth where it lay.

It swelled even bigger – and then it put out a little root, a thin white thread. A worm came by and looked at it, but he did not eat the small seed.

The root grew well. It felt its way down into the earth and grew tiny little hairs all along its length. Then more roots grew.

'What are those white threads for?' said the worm when he came by that way again.

'For holding on,' said the tiny seed. 'I don't want to wriggle about like you do. I want to sit down and hold on tight.'

Then one day out came a tiny little shoot from the seed. It didn't feel its way downwards as the roots did. It wanted to go upwards. It longed to get into the daylight and feel the warm sun.

At last its little green head poked out from the earth. 'Who are you?' said the grass. 'We don't want anyone else here. There's no room for you!'

'I'm a daisy plant,' said the tiny shoot. 'Let me

grow up, please. Surely there is room for a tiny thing like me?'

'Ah, but you won't stay tiny!' said the whispering grass. 'We shall try to squash you! We won't give you room to grow!'

And so the grass grew as closely together as it could, all the little green blades pressing over the tiny daisy shoot.

'You are unkind,' said the daisy plant. 'I am so small. You should help me!'

But the grass would not help it. It did its best to squeeze it out. Still the little shoot grew, and one day it had two tiny leaves!

'Now you can't stop me,' said the daisy. 'I'm a tiny plant. I have roots and two leaves. I shall grow and grow. My roots will hold me down safely, and they will drink up the raindrops when they come, so that I shall not be thirsty.'

'You are not to grow any bigger!' said the grass. 'Already you have pushed us a little to one side. There is no room for you on this lawn! Someone will come and dig you up, daisy. People only like grass on a lawn.'

'You can't stop me!' said the daisy again and, hey presto, four more leaves grew. Now it had six spreading out from each side, and soon more would grow.

'We shall not make room for you!' said the grass, and they pressed so closely round the daisy that it had to lift up its leaves.

A bumblebee flew by. 'Why, here's a new little daisy plant!' he said. 'Daisy, why do you lift your leaves so high?'

'Because the grass won't give me room,' said the daisy.

'I'll tell you how to make room for yourself!' said the bee, humming loudly. 'Press your leaves down flat, daisy. Grow them in a circle round you!'

So the daisy pressed her leaves flat all round her, squeezing down on the grass blades.

'You are squashing us!' said the grass. 'Get away, daisy.'

'No. I shall sit here,' said the daisy. 'I shall press down my leaves in a tight little circle, and make my own place to sit in. You tried to squeeze me so that I would not be able to grow. Now I am making my own home to sit in!'

And there it sat, its leaves in a firm rosette round it, and took no notice of the grass. Soon buds formed in the middle of the rosette. They grew stalks, hairy little stalks that held the round, tight little buds.

The sun shone down warmly, and the buds opened. Each daisy had one big golden eye in the middle of its pretty circle of white florets.

'How sweet you are!' said a little elf, running up. 'See, I have a tin of pink paint. Shall I paint the tips of your white florets red?'

'Yes,' said the daisy, pleased. But because the elf could hardly reach the flower, he only painted the under-tips red. They showed well when the daisies closed up at night.

'Ha!' said a loud voice one day, and heavy footsteps

sounded on the lawn. 'A daisy in my lovely lawn! Here, Angela, dig it out for me with this little fork.'

'Oh, no, Daddy! It's so pretty!' said Angela. 'And it must have had such a hard task, making room for itself in the middle of all this closely growing grass. Look at the pink tips – who painted those, I wonder?'

So there the daisy still sits, in the middle of Angela's lawn. 'This is my place!' it says to the grass. 'I shall sit here!'

Your daisies say the same. Go and see how they all sit tightly on your lawn!

Pixie Mirrors

Pixie Mirrors

IN CLARA'S garden, though Clara didn't know it, lived a whole family of curly-headed pixies. They were the prettiest things, as light as thistledown, and as merry as a blackbird in spring.

Everybody liked them. The fieldmice who lived in the meadow at the bottom of the garden often asked them to tea, and the larks in the field took them to see their young ones as soon as they were out of the egg.

The meadow pixies asked them to dances, and even the cross old goblin who lived inside the hollow oak tree used to poke his head out and smile at them if he heard the flutter of their small wings going by.

Now whenever they were asked out to a party the curly-headed pixies used to dress themselves up in their best blue-and-silver dresses, and brush out their hair till it shone like a golden mist around their small heads.

And then they used to fly to Clara's bedroom window, creep in very quietly, and go to Clara's mirror. It stood on her dressing table, and was very pretty, for it had flowers all round it.

Each pixie took her turn at looking in to see if her dress was right and her hair was neat. They patted their skirts down and dabbed at their curly hair, chattering excitedly all the time.

And Clara never knew! She didn't guess that the pixies used her mirror for their own, though once, on a rainy night, she was puzzled to find a whole crowd of tiny muddy footsteps on her clean white dressing table cover!

Can it be the cat? she thought. *No, cats don't have such small feet, nor such pointed toes either. It's very odd.*

And then one day a dreadful thing happened. Clara went to put some flowers on her dressing table, and her hand knocked against the mirror. It fell over, slid off the dressing table and then fell to the ground with a crash! Bits of broken glass flew around Clara's feet.

'Oh my goodness! Look at that!' cried Clara in dismay. 'My lovely, lovely mirror is broken! Mother, look what I've done!'

Mother was sad. It had been such a beautiful mirror. 'Never mind,' she said. 'Maybe we can get a new glass fitted into it and then it will be all right again. But you have broken one or two of the flowers off too, Clara. I wonder if those can be mended.'

'That's seven years' bad luck for Clara,' said Jane the maid, looking in at the bedroom door.

'Don't be silly, Jane,' said Mother. 'Bad luck has nothing whatever to do with breaking a mirror. It's bad luck to *break* a mirror certainly – but, really, I didn't think you still believed that silly old tale of seven years' bad luck!'

Jane went away blushing. Clara swept up the broken bits of mirror and put them into the dustbin. Mother took the broken mirror to see if it could be mended.

So Clara had no mirror on her dressing table to tell her if she was neat and tidy.

Well, it's a good thing no one else uses the mirror but me, thought Clara.

That was just where she was wrong! The curly-headed pixies had a great disappointment when they came along that evening to see if they were looking pretty for a dance that the cross old goblin was giving especially for them. There was no mirror there!

'It's gone!' said one.

'Let's look for it!' said another.

But that wasn't any good, because it just wasn't anywhere in the room at all. The pixies were so busy looking for it that they didn't hear Clara come into the room, and the little girl stood staring in surprise and joy at the twelve tiny pixies flying all around her bedroom!

'Am I dreaming?' she cried. 'Or are you real?'

The pixies flew together in a bunch, looking round in fright. Then one of them spoke.

'We are real, of course,' she said. 'We were looking for your mirror, Clara. We always came to peep in it before we went to a party. But now it's gone.'

'It's broken,' said Clara sadly. 'Did you badly want to see yourselves, pixies? There is a long mirror in my mother's room. You can peep into that if you like.'

'No, thank you,' said the pixies at once. 'We shouldn't really have let *you* see us, Clara – we would get into trouble if we let a grown-up see us. Oh, dear, what are we to do? There is no pond in the garden to look into.'

'Shall I tell you something?' said Clara suddenly. 'Well, listen. This afternoon when I went down the garden, it had been raining. And as I passed by the lupin plants I saw such a pretty sight. One of the lupin leaves had curved its pretty green leaflets upwards and had caught a bright raindrop just in the middle! I am sure you could find it and use it for a mirror!'

'That *is* an idea!' cried the pixies in delight. 'We'll go and find it straight away, Clara.'

They flew out of the window. They went to where the blue and pink lupins grew. They had pretty leaves cut up into green fingers and, sure enough, in the centre of one was a bright raindrop, just big enough to make a little mirror for the curly-headed pixies! One by one they looked into it, and patted their hair and arranged their dresses. It was just right for them!

Then a pixie knocked against the lupin leaf and the raindrop rolled out and splashed on to the ground. The little lupin mirror was broken!

But it didn't matter. The pixies had finished with it, and went off gaily to their dance. They had a lovely time, and told everyone about the funny little mirror they had found in the lupins.

Clara's mirror was mended and was put back on her

dressing table, but the pixies never used it again, though they often remembered Clara and dropped fresh flowers on to her pillow for her to find.

They asked the lupin leaves to hold the raindrops for them whenever it rained – and that is just what they do. They make beautiful mirrors for the little folk, and are simply lovely to see. You won't forget to look for them, will you, after a rain shower? You will find those pixie mirrors gleaming brightly here and there in the centre of the lupin leaves. Roll one out and see it break on the bed below!

Muddlesome's Mistake

Muddlesome's Mistake

ONCE UPON a time there was a gnome who was too conceited for anything. He was the only person in his town who took a newspaper, so, of course, he knew the news before anyone else did. The thing that interested him more than anything was the little bit that told him what the weather was going to be that day.

He used to read this every morning, and then he would go out into the marketplace and tell all the gnomes, brownies, elves and fairies what the weather was going to be. He didn't tell them that he got it all from the newspaper, because he wanted them to think

97

he was very clever and could tell the weather out of his own head.

The little folk used to listen, but behind his back they laughed at him, because he was so vain. Still, they thought it really was very wonderful of him to be able to say, 'Today it will be fine and warm, without rain,' or 'Today it will be stormy, and the wind will change to the west.'

'How do you know, Muddlesome?' they often asked him.

'Oh, I can tell by the clouds and the wind and the air, and things like that,' said Muddlesome untruthfully, though he knew perfectly well that he had learnt the weather off by heart that very morning from the newspaper.

Now one day Pippin, the chief gnome of the village, made up his mind to give a garden party.

'I'll give it on Saturday,' he decided, 'and I'll ask everyone in the village to it. But first I'll go round to Muddlesome and ask him if the weather will be fine.'

So he popped round to Muddlesome's cottage and asked him.

'Well, I can't tell you until Saturday comes,' said Muddlesome, most delighted to think that the chief gnome should ask his advice. 'I'll tell you what I'll do, Pippin, I'll come round at nine o'clock on Saturday morning, and tell you if it will be fine or not. Then you can put everything out in the garden if it is going to be fine, and indoors if I say it will be wet.'

So it was settled like that, and all the invitations went out that afternoon.

Now when Saturday came Muddlesome's newspaper was put through the letterbox as usual. He was just in the middle of making himself very smart to go round to Pippin's, so he ran to fetch it, and popped it into the newspaper rack until he was ready to look at it. Then he went to finish dressing.

After that he had his breakfast, and while he was eating bread and marmalade and drinking cocoa, he opened his newspaper and propped it up before him.

'Now what's the weather going to be?' he wondered. 'Ha! Here it is! "Very fine and warm. Southerly breeze, no rain." How pleased Pippin will be! He can have his party in the garden quite safely.'

At half past nine he hurried round to Pippin's.

'Hallo,' said Pippin dolefully. 'This looks as if it's going to be a very bad day, doesn't it?' And he pointed to the black cloudy sky.

'Nonsense,' said Muddlesome briskly. 'It's going to be very fine and warm, with southerly breezes and no rain.'

'But, Muddlesome, are you sure?' asked Pippin in surprise. 'It's a west wind now, and that brings rain, you know. And *I* think it's very cold.'

'Rubbish!' said Muddlesome. 'You can quite safely put everything in the garden, Pippin. I tell you I can't make a mistake.'

'How do you know all this about the weather?' asked Pippin.

'Oh, I tell by the sky and the way the wind feels

on my cheek,' said Muddlesome grandly. 'You will be perfectly safe to put everything out, I tell you, Pippin.'

So Pippin believed him, and had all the tables and chairs placed in the garden, and put the cakes and jellies, buns and sandwiches, ice creams and strawberries out too. And then, just as the guests arrived, the rain began!

You should have seen it pour down! It simply pelted on to the cakes and ices, and then the wind got up and blew the tables and chairs over. After that the thunder came and the lightning, and everyone crowded into Pippin's tiny house in a fright. It was a terrible thing to happen on a garden party day.

Pippin was very angry with Muddlesome.

'Didn't I tell you it would rain?' he shouted. 'What do you mean by saying it was going to be fine and warm, and all that nonsense, Muddlesome? I've a good mind to punish you!'

'Poor old Pippin!' cried everyone. 'It's a shame!

Yes, punish him, Pippin! There's all your lovely things spoilt because of that horrid Muddlesome!'

'Please, please,' begged Muddlesome, getting frightened. 'It was the paper that told me about the weather today. I didn't make it up, really I didn't.'

'Oh, so you told a story to me, did you?' said Pippin. 'You told me you found out about the weather all by yourself! Just run home in the rain and fetch that newspaper.'

So Muddlesome ran home and fetched it. He showed Pippin what it said: *Fine and warm. Southerly breeze, and no rain.*

Then Pippin looked closely at the paper and said, 'You are a great stupid, Muddlesome. This is yesterday's paper, and that was yesterday's weather. Just go and fetch today's, and let us read that.'

So Muddlesome went to fetch today's, puzzling to know how he could have read the wrong paper. Then he remembered how he had put the morning's paper with the others in the newspaper rack, and knew that he must have taken the wrong one out to read at breakfast time!

Sure enough, that was what he had done! And when the silly little gnome read that day's weather, this is what he saw: *Very cold. Westerly wind, with much rain. Stormy in afternoon, with strong winds blowing.*

'Oh, oh!' he groaned miserably. 'I daren't go and face everyone with this! How they will laugh at me! No one will think I'm clever any more! And Pippin will be sure to be cross with me for spoiling his lovely party! I shall run away, that's what I shall do!'

He was as good as his word. He packed a bag quickly, and caught the first bus out of the village, while all the guests in Pippin's house wondered what had become of him.

And no one has heard of him to this day, which, as Pippin said, is quite a good thing, for who wants to be friends with a vain and conceited gnome like Muddlesome?

Sally's Umbrella

Sally's Umbrella

'SALLY!' CALLED her mother. 'I want you to go to the newspaper shop for me and fetch me my magazine.'

'Must I?' called back Sally. 'It looks as if it's going to pour with rain, Mummy.'

'Well, take your umbrella then,' said her mother. 'I gave you a lovely one for your birthday. You ought to be pleased to use it.'

'Mummy, my shoes let in the wet,' said Sally, trying to think of another excuse not to go.

'Well, put on your Wellington boots then, if your shoes want mending,' said Mother. 'Here's threepence. Now you go along at once, before the shop shuts.

Your umbrella and your boots are in the hall cupboard. Hurry, Sally.'

Sally took the threepence. Bother! Now she would have to go – and she did so badly want to finish her book.

She put on her boots. She put on her coat. She took her umbrella. She held the money in her hand and she set off.

Well, it began to pour with rain, just as Sally had thought it would. How it pelted down! She put up her umbrella and trotted down the road, hoping there would soon be puddles she could splash through. Her mother didn't mind her doing that if she had her boots on.

The rain stopped very suddenly. Sally put down her umbrella. She came to the newspaper shop and walked in.

'Can I have Mummy's magazine, please?' she said. But when she wanted to pay for it the threepence wasn't in her hand. It was gone.

'Oh, dear – I must have dropped it,' said Sally, and back she went, hunting along the road for the penny. But it was quite gone.

She went home, upset. 'I've lost the money, Mummy,' she said. 'I'm so sorry. I didn't hear it drop or I would have known I'd lost it. I can't imagine where it is!'

'That's careless of you, Sally,' said her mother. 'Here's another threepence. Now don't you dare to come back and say you've lost that one too!'

'Of course not,' said Sally, and she set off again, holding the money tightly in her hand, and the umbrella in the other. It wasn't raining any more, so she didn't need to have it up this time.

She splashed through a puddle and made such a shower of drops that some went down into her boots. 'Oh, dear,' she said, and looked to see if her socks were wet. They didn't seem to be. She walked on to the shop – and, would you believe it, when she got there she hadn't got the threepence again! She stared at her empty hand in dismay.

'Well! Your mother won't be at all pleased with you!' said the shopkeeper, and put the magazine back on the shelf again.

Sally nearly cried. This was most mysterious. Another threepence gone! Well, she must have dropped it by that big puddle she splashed through. That's where it must have gone.

So back she went to the puddle. She looked into it. She looked all round it. She looked in the road and by the side of the road. No threepence.

'Bother! Somebody must have come by and picked it up,' said poor Sally, and went home very slowly indeed, afraid that Mother would be crosser than ever.

But she wasn't. She was sorry to see Sally's frightened, upset little face. She patted her.

'Never mind! It was my fault for sending you shopping with money. You're too little to take care of it yet.'

'I'm not, really,' Sally said in a small voice. 'I kept them both carefully – and then they just disappeared.

I'm sure I didn't drop them. I would have heard them if I had. It must be a magic spell, Mummy.'

'In that case, they'll probably come back again,' said Mother. 'We'll hope so anyway! Now put your coat on again, because Granny has just phoned to say will we go and have lunch with her today. We'll go now.'

Well, that was nice. It was always fun to go to Granny's. Sally set off with her mother, carrying her umbrella in case it rained again. But it didn't.

They got to Granny's. She was at the front door, waiting for them. She smiled when she saw them.

'Well, well, here's little Sally with her new umbrella!' she said. 'Let's have a look at it, Sally!' She took it and opened it – and, dear me, down on the top of Granny's head fell a threepence. She was most surprised.

'Oh!' squealed Sally. 'There's one of the threepences, Mummy. It was down the umbrella! Oh, I'm so glad!'

'Well, now perhaps the other will turn up,' said her

mother, laughing. 'Come along, we must go in.'

'Take off your boots first, Sally,' said Granny. 'Shall I pull them off for you?' She pulled one boot off, and then the other. And out of the second one shot a threepence!

'Well, goodness gracious, child, are you made of pennies?' cried Granny.

'Mummy! Mummy! The other threepence was in my boot!' squealed Sally. 'I didn't lose that one either.'

Well, wasn't that peculiar? Sally couldn't help thinking that there might be some magic about. One threepence in her umbrella, and the other in her boots – very strange.

And, would you believe it, when she got home she felt in her pocket – and there was another one there too! That was very extraordinary, because Sally knew she had only had her hanky there when she set out to Granny's.

'There *is* magic about,' she said happily. 'So you can't blame me for losing the money any more,

Mummy. I can't help it if there's magic about.'

But I shouldn't be surprised if Granny had popped that threepence in her pocket for a surprise, would you? It's the sort of thing grannies do – the nice ones anyway!

Mr Stamp-About
Goes Shopping

Mr Stamp-About
Goes Shopping

MR STAMP-ABOUT stalked into Mr Tidy the tailor's shop and banged on the counter.

'I want to be served!' he said. 'I'm in a hurry!'

Mr Tidy turned from the customer he was serving. 'Just a minute, sir,' he said. 'I'll come to you as soon as I've finished helping this gentleman.'

'I want serving now,' said Stamp-About rudely.

'Very well, sir,' said Mr Tidy, and called to the back of the shop. 'Forward, please, Button!'

Out hurried a scared-looking boy, with a button in one hand and a needle in the other. 'I'm just sewing on those buttons, sir,' he said. 'Did you want me?'

'Yes. Serve this gentleman,' said Mr Tidy, and poor little Button looked in alarm at the fierce Mr Stamp-About.

'I will not be served by this little shrimp!' said Mr Stamp-About angrily.

'Well, sir, I haven't any lobsters serving in the shop today,' said Mr Tidy apologetically. That made his customer laugh loudly, and little Button giggled in delight.

Stamp-About stamped his foot and began to roar. 'I'm in a hurry! I've got to go to a grand luncheon party and I want a new coat and hat and umbrella – *at once*!'

'Show him some coats, Button,' said Mr Tidy, and with trembling hands poor Button took down some coats from a rail.

Mr Stamp-About tried them on, grumbling all the time.

'Awful colour! Shocking pattern! What a collar! Look at these pockets! And the price – my word, what robbers you are here!'

'Well, would you like to fetch the policeman?' asked Mr Tidy, getting a bit tired of Stamp-About. 'He's always interested in robbers. Look, he's just outside, across the street.'

But Stamp-About didn't fetch him. He knew that the policeman wasn't very fond of him! He tried on more coats, and then called for hats.

'Silly hats! All too small!' he said.

'You have a rather big head, sir,' said Mr Tidy. 'Look, there's a good hat, there. The largest size we have. Put it on his head, Button.'

Button carefully fitted it on Stamp-About's head. It was just his size, and a very nice hat indeed.

'Hmm. Not bad,' said Stamp-About, turning his head this way and that to see the hat better. 'Yes, I'll have it, if it's not too much money. Now, what about an umbrella – and after that I'll decide on a coat.'

Button gave him one. 'Not bad,' said Stamp-About and opened it so suddenly that Button fell over backwards. 'Now where's that little shrimp gone?

Hey! What are you squatting on the floor for? Get up at once!'

In the end Stamp-About chose a coat, a hat and an umbrella – but how he argued about the price! 'If I buy three things I ought to have them cheap,' he said, and began to stamp about the shop, calling Mr Tidy a robber and a thief until the poor man got so tired of him that he gave way. Anything to get Stamp-About out of his shop! He was scaring other customers away.

'Very well, I will take a shilling off the price,' said Mr Tidy. 'Button, wrap up the things, then Mr Stamp-About can go.'

'No, don't wrap them up,' said Stamp-About. 'I want to wear them. I told you I'm going to a grand luncheon party. Here's the money and I still think you're robbing me, charging so much even though you took a shilling off the price.'

Mr Tidy said nothing. He was sure he would lose his temper if he had much more of Stamp-About. Little Button tremblingly helped him into his new coat, and gave him the new hat and the new umbrella. Then he scampered into the back of the shop, and sat down thankfully to his task of sewing on buttons.

Stamp-About went out of the shop without so much as a thank-you. He muttered crossly as he went. 'Robbers! What a price to pay for new clothes!'

He was on his way to Mr High-Up who was giving the party in his very grand house on the other side of the town. Stamp-About decided to take a short cut through the woods. Just then the wind got up and tugged at his hat, and he had to hold it on tightly.

'Stop it, wind!' he said. 'Can't you see I'm wearing a new hat? I don't want it blown into the wood. Behave yourself!'

But the wind was going to do as it liked. It waited till Stamp-About was in the wood and then it pounced on him and blew his new hat right off his head, and what was more it blew it high up into a tree!

Stamp-About lost his temper and roared at the wind, and stamped round the tree. 'How dare you!

That's my new hat! Blow it down to me at once! Shake yourself, tree, and throw down my hat!'

But the hat didn't stir from the tree. It hung up there on a small branch and jiggled a little in the wind.

'All right. I'll come up and get you,' said Mr Stamp-About. 'But I'd better take off my grand new coat, else I shall tear it on a branch. And I'll stand my new umbrella beside it too.'

So he took off his coat and laid it carefully on a tree stump not far off. He stood his umbrella beside it. Then back he went to the tree and began to climb it. It was a difficult tree to climb and little bits and pieces kept catching at him as he climbed. He felt very cross indeed. What a long way up his hat was!

Just as he got almost to the hat at the top of the tree the wind pounced down again and blew so hard that the tree rocked from side to side. It made a loud rustling noise, and Stamp-About very nearly fell out. He clung to a bough for all he was worth.

Now, down in the wood below, was a little old man. He was very poor, and had come to pick up wood for his fire. He came up to the tree stump where Stamp-About had put his coat and umbrella, and stared at them in surprise. Why were they there? Whose were they? Had someone left them there because he didn't want them any more? But the coat seemed a very good one – and the umbrella was a beauty!

'Does anyone own these?' shouted the old man. But nobody answered. Stamp-About was being blown about in the tree and he didn't hear a thing.

'Well, well, it seems a pity to leave them here to rot in the wind and rain,' said the old fellow. 'I can sell them for quite a bit of money.'

So he picked them up and went off with them, wearing the coat and swinging the umbrella, feeling very grand.

Now who will buy these? he thought. *Yes, I'll go to old Tidy the tailor's. He's a nice fellow. He'll give me a fair price for them.*

But when he got to Mr Tidy's shop, the tailor was just going off to his lunch. He called to little Button. 'Hey, Button, see to this man for me, will you? He says he's got secondhand clothes to sell. Give him a fair price.' And off went Mr Tidy.

Button was astonished to see the coat and umbrella. *They can't be the ones I sold this morning, because that awful Mr Stamp-About went off in them*, he thought. *And he certainly wouldn't give them away almost at once.*

'Will you buy them?' asked the old fellow. 'The coat is quite good, you know, and so is the umbrella.'

'Yes, I know,' said Button. 'We sell the same things ourselves. I will give you half the price we charge when they are new. That's fair enough.'

'Very fair!' said the old man in delight. 'Ah, I can see sausages for my supper every night this week and a fire in my kitchen and hot cocoa before I go to bed. That's what money means to me, young Button! I'll take it now.'

He went off happily with the money, and jingled

it in his pocket all the way to the sausage shop. What luck!

Button went back to his job of sewing on buttons but he hadn't been working for more than ten minutes when he heard a loud roaring outside the shop. Gracious, had a lion escaped from a zoo? Button ran behind a rail of coats and trembled.

But it wasn't a lion. It was only a very, very angry Mr Stamp-About. He came stamping into the shop and roared for Mr Tidy.

'He's gone to his lunch,' said Button, peering out fearfully from behind the coats. 'There's only me here.'

'Oh, the shrimp!' said Stamp-About rudely. 'Well, look here, someone's stolen that new coat and umbrella I bought this morning – the wind blew my hat up a tree and while I was climbing to fetch it, a thief came along and took my coat and umbrella.'

Button immediately felt certain that the thief was the old man who had just sold him a coat and umbrella, and he was very frightened.

'Oh, sir,' he began, 'an old man came in just now and—'

'Don't interrupt me when I'm talking,' said Stamp-About angrily. 'I tell you, when I came down the tree—'

'But, sir, I'm sure that the old man who—' said Button earnestly, and once more Stamp-About cut him short.

'Stop talking about old men! Show me a coat exactly like the one I bought this morning, and an umbrella. I shall be ruined, having to buy them, but I simply must go well dressed to this party. After all, I am the great Mr Stamp-About.'

'Yes, sir,' said Button, not daring to say any more about the old man. 'Well, I'm afraid we haven't a coat or umbrella like the ones you bought this morning, sir.'

'You storyteller!' cried Stamp-About angrily, and pointed to the coat and umbrella that the old man had just sold to Button. 'There's a coat like mine, and an umbrella too. How dare you tell such untruths? I'll take those, and you'll have to take a shilling off the price just as you did this morning.'

'But, sir – do listen, sir,' began poor Button desperately, and then gave a yell as Stamp-About picked up the umbrella and chased him round and round the shop with it, shouting all the time. Goodness, what a man!

'All right. Take the coat and the umbrella,' yelled Button from behind the counter. 'Leave the money over there. Don't you come near me again!'

With a loud snort Stamp-About put the money down, took the coat and umbrella and went stamping out of the shop. Button sank down on a chair and wondered what Mr Tidy would say to him when he knew that he had sold Mr Stamp-About the same coat and umbrella that he had already bought that morning. Would he be very angry?

No, he wasn't! When he heard poor Button's tale he sat down on a chair and laughed till the tears ran down his cheeks. 'Oh my word!' he chuckled. 'To think that you were clever enough to sell the old rascal his things all over again! Well, he wouldn't listen to your explanations, so it's his own fault. You can have half the money yourself, Button. You had to pay half price to the old man for the things, so you can put half the money back into the till and keep the rest yourself.'

'Oh, thank you, sir!' said Button. 'That will make up for all the frights he gave me. Thank you very much! Whatever would Mr Stamp-About say if he knew he had paid twice for the same things?'

Well, I can guess! But as nobody will ever tell him it won't matter. It was a very expensive morning for him, wasn't it?

Pinkity's Pranks

Pinkity's Pranks

ONCE UPON a time there lived a naughty little pixie called Pinkity. He was always in mischief, and teased everyone he met.

Now, what shall I do today? thought Pinkity, as he sat in a may bush and swung his legs. *I know – I'll get my little watering can and water all the people who walk in the wood!*

He flew to get it, and filled it with water. Then he perched himself up in his tree again and waited.

Presently along came Dwarf Yellow Buttons, carrying his lovely new mackintosh, who walked just underneath Pinkity's tree.

Splish-splash! Splish-splash!

Down went the water from Pinkity's can, all over Dwarf Yellow Buttons!

'Dear, dear, dear!' cried Dwarf Yellow Buttons, hastily putting on his mackintosh. 'Who would have thought it would rain so soon?'

Pinkity laughed and laughed to see Yellow Buttons running off into the sunshine with his mackintosh on!

Presently came the Lord High Chancellor of Fairyland, talking earnestly with the prince of Dreamland.

Splish-splash! Splish-splash!

Down came the water over them!

'Why, bless me!' cried the chancellor, hurriedly putting up a large red umbrella. 'Fancy it raining like this! I hope you're not wet, Your Highness!'

'Yes, I am,' said the prince, 'and I don't believe it's rain; I believe it's a trick. See, the sun is shining yonder!'

Then the chancellor heard Pinkity laughing, and he looked up into the may bush.

'You bad, mischievous little pixie!' he cried in a great rage. 'I'll catch you and take you to the king.'

But Pinkity flew off in a great hurry, and was soon lost to sight. He was just a bit frightened, and for a little while he was quite good.

He wandered over the fields, and suddenly saw someone lying down fast asleep and snoring by the hedge.

He crept up to look.

'It's old Togs the tailor!' he said to himself in great delight. 'I'll borrow his big scissors for a little while.'

So Pinkity took the tailor's scissors and flew off with them, looking for something to cut and snip.

Now in the next field were a lot of fairy sheep with their little lambs.

'Hallo!' said Pinkity, flying up to them. 'Look what I've got! Old Togs the tailor's scissors!'

'Oh, Pinkity, *do* cut off our heavy tails!' begged the lambs, crowding round him. 'They're so hot, and they knock against our legs so.'

'But you're not supposed to have them cut off till next month,' said Pinkity, longing to snip them off.

'Never mind! Cut them off *now*! Oh, do, Pinkity, dear, dear Pinkity,' begged the lambs.

'All right, I'd love to!' answered the naughty little pixie. 'Come here, Long-Legs, I'll do you first!'

Little Long-Legs frisked up, and snip! snip! went the big scissors.

'There,' said Pinkity. 'I've cut your tail off. Do you feel cooler?'

'Oh, yes, yes,' said the lamb, skipping away in delight. 'That's *much* better!'

'Come along, Frisky, let me do yours,' laughed Pinkity, waving his big scissors.

One by one each of the little lambs came up to Pinkity and had its long, heavy tail cut off. Soon the grass was covered with little tails, and Pinkity's arm began to ache.

'There!' he said as he cut off the very last one. 'There! That's all! Now I'll give Togs the tailor his scissors.'

Pinkity flew off and put the big scissors down by Togs the tailor, who was still asleep, and then made friends with two bumblebees, who gave him a good feast of honey for his dinner.

Soon he heard a great noise, and flew into the fields to see what it was.

He saw the Lord High Chancellor of Fairyland in the fields shaking Togs the tailor angrily and scolding him.

'What do you mean by cutting off the lambs' tails?' he roared. 'Don't you know they are never cut until next month? How dare you!'

'I didn't, Your Highness, I didn't!' said poor old Togs, the tears running down his cheeks. 'I wouldn't do such a thing, really and truly I wouldn't!'

Pinkity felt very much upset. He knew he had done something naughty, and he wasn't very sorry about it, but he couldn't bear to see poor old Togs punished for something he hadn't done.

He flew straight down into the field, and knelt

before the astonished Lord Chancellor.

'Please, Your Highness,' he cried, 'don't punish Togs. *I* took his scissors while he was asleep and cut the lambs' tails off.'

The chancellor let Togs go and stared at Pinkity.

'Oho!' he said. 'You're the pixie who poured water on us this morning! Come here!

'Although you're naughty,' he said, 'I am pleased that you came and owned up when I was scolding Togs for something *you* had done. I shan't punish you for cutting off the lambs' tails, but I shall see that you always have work to do now, instead of flying about all day and playing tricks.'

'Let him clear up all these lambs' tails,' said Togs the tailor.

'Yes, I will. Go and hang them on the hazelnut trees, Pinkity. They want cheering up a bit. And, mind, if you play any more tricks, I'll punish you again! Now off you go!'

Off went naughty little Pinkity, carrying an

armful of lambs' tails. He hung them on the hazelnut twigs, and very pretty they looked too, all shaking in the wind.

Pinkity is still sometimes naughty, but he's so busy, especially in springtime, that he doesn't find time for *many* tricks.

And if you look on the hazel trees you will find the little lambs' tails hanging there, and if your eyes are extra sharp, you *might* see Pinkity flying from twig to twig, watching them shake and wiggle in the wind, just as they did when they grew on the little fairy lambs!

Rain in Toytown

Rain in Toytown

ONCE UPON a time there was a big toy duck who sat on a shelf in the toyshop and was never sold.

He had been pushed behind a big box, and no one knew he was there. He was really a fine duck. He was made of celluloid, and if only he had been put into a bath full of water, then you would have seen how beautifully he could float! But ever since he had been in the shop he had sat up on the dark shelf and had never moved from there – he did not even know that he could float!

He had no legs, so he could not get up and walk about at nights as the other toys did. All he could do was to poke his big orange beak out from behind the box, and watch the other toys dancing, shouting and playing together on the floor below.

So you can guess he led a very dull life and was always longing for a little excitement, which never came.

And then one day a doll with a barrow was put up on the shelf near the duck! The wheel of the barrow had broken, so the doll could not be sold. It went by clockwork and when it was wound up it walked along, holding the barrow and pushing it. It was lovely to watch it. But now that the wheel was broken the toy did not work properly and the doll was no use either.

'Hallo!' said the duck in great surprise. 'I haven't seen anyone up on this shelf for years! How did you get here?'

'I've been put up here out of the way,' said the doll sadly. 'I expect I shall be here for years too, getting older and dustier each day!'

'I am dusty too,' said the duck. 'You would not

think that my back was really a bright blue, green and red, would you? Well, it is! But there is so much dust on me that I look grey. I have kept my beak a nice bright orange by rubbing it against the back of this box. Oh, doll, it is so exciting to have someone to talk to!'

'Do you suppose everyone will forget about me, as they have forgotten about you?' asked the doll, with tears in her blue eyes.

She was a dear little doll, with a pretty face and shining fair hair. Her hands held the handles of the barrow tightly.

'I expect we shall stay here till we fall to pieces,' said the duck with a sigh.

'Well, I don't see why we should!' said the doll, tossing back her hair fiercely. 'Surely we can think of a way to escape from this shelf.'

'But where should we go if we did?' said the duck. 'You would be put back on the shelf, if the shopkeeper found you again, I am sure.'

'If only I could mend my wheel, I could wheel my barrow away and go to Toytown,' sighed the doll. 'I know the way quite well.'

'Let me have a look at the wheel,' begged the duck. 'Perhaps I can think of a way of mending it!'

The doll pulled the barrow round so that the duck could see it. Part of the wheel was actually missing. There was no mending it, that was certain!

'I believe I know what you could do!' said the duck in excitement. 'Why not take out that wheel and slip in something else instead – a cotton reel, for instance? That would make a very strong wheel!'

'I didn't think of that!' cried the doll. 'Oh, duck, that would be just the thing! Tonight I will see what I can do!' So that night the doll tried to get out the broken wheel. The duck helped her by pecking hard, and at last out came the wheel!

'Good!' cried the duck. 'Now climb down to the workbasket on that chair, doll. You are sure to find an empty reel there.'

The doll climbed down. The basket belonged to the shop girl, and in it she had full reels, half-used ones and two empty ones. The doll chose the bigger one of the two, and climbed back to the shelf with it. The duck helped her fit it into the barrow – and, hey presto, she could wheel it along beautifully! The reel went round and round just as well as the wheel had done.

'And now I shall go to Toytown,' said the doll happily, taking hold of the handles of the barrow.

'Well, goodbye,' said the duck sadly. 'I am glad you are able to go, but I am sorry to lose you.'

'Oh, but you are coming with me!' said the doll, laughing.

'How can I do that?' cried the duck. 'I have no legs, and cannot walk, and my wings are only painted. They will not fly.'

'Ah, but I shall put you into my barrow and wheel you along with me!' said the kind little doll. 'You have helped me, duck, and now I will help you.

You are not heavy, and though you will not fit very well into my barrow, still, I think I can manage!'

The duck was too excited to answer! The doll picked him up in her arms, for he was very light, though quite big. She put him on her barrow – he would not go right in for he was too big, but she managed to balance him quite well. Then she wheeled him to the end of the shelf.

Just below the shelf stood a big doll's house. The doll cleverly wheeled the barrow from the shelf to the roof of the house, then down the roof to a balcony that jutted out from a bedroom. Then she called to a big teddy bear, and asked him to help her.

'Will you lift down this duck for me, and my barrow?' she asked. 'I can quite well climb down myself.'

The big bear was a good-natured fellow, and he lifted down the duck gently, and then the barrow. The cotton reel fell out and the bear pushed it in again. The doll quickly climbed down from the balcony and put the duck in the barrow. They called 'thank you and goodbye' to the teddy bear, and then off they went on the way to Toytown, the doll wheeling the duck in the barrow.

They journeyed for two nights and a day, and at last they came to Toytown. At the gates stood a wooden policeman

'What do you want in Toytown?' he asked. 'It is very full just now. Unless you have some work to do, doll and duck, I cannot let you in.'

'I'm a gardener doll,' said the little doll. 'Can't you see my barrow and my overall? I'm a very good gardener; I shall soon find work to do.'

'But what about the duck?' asked the policeman. 'What work will he do?'

'Oh, he'll find something!' said the doll. 'Do let me in, please, for I am very tired.'

So, grumbling a little, the toy policeman let them go through the gates, and the wheelbarrow rumbled down the neat streets of Toytown. Doll's houses stood on every side, and toyshops sold their wares. Little farms with wooden animals and trees were here and there. The doll stopped at the gate of one.

'I think I'll go in and ask the farmer here if he will let me be his gardener,' said the doll. 'I can see one or two trees that have fallen over, and a pond that you could float on!'

So she wheeled her barrow, and the duck as well, through the farm gate and went up to the farmer. He was made of wood, and he had very sharp eyes.

'Oh, so you want to be a gardener here, do you?' he said. 'Well, I can do with one. I have too much work to do. Can you feed the chickens and the ducks too, and look after the pigs as well?'

'Oh, yes,' said the doll. 'I can do anything. Will you please let the duck in my barrow float on your pond until he too finds some work to do?'

'Very well,' said the farmer. 'Take him over there.'

So the duck was taken to a small pond and he floated there in great delight. The pond was very tiny, and the duck almost filled it all. When he floated very hard he made big waves at the edge of the pond and then all the tiny ducks nearby quacked with fright.

The doll set to work. She was a good gardener, and she did her best to see to the chickens, ducks and pigs too. She enjoyed working in the sunshine, but when it began to rain and her hair and overall got soaked she did not like it so much.

'My feet get stuck in the mud,' she complained to the duck. 'It is horrid!'

The duck liked the rain. For one thing it made his pond bigger, and that gave him more room. He liked to feel the raindrops too – but he was sorry for the little doll.

'Have you found me any work to do yet?' he asked the doll.

'No,' said the doll with a sigh. 'It seems very difficult to get work for someone who cannot walk or fly. I am worried about you, duck. The policeman said yesterday that the little ducklings here complained that you take up all the room on their pond. He said that you will have to leave Toytown next week if you cannot get any work.'

'Oh, dear!' said the duck in dismay. 'That means I shall have to go back to that horrid shelf for the rest of my life!'

'I don't want you to do that,' said the doll with tears in her eyes. 'I am so fond of you now. And you do look so beautiful since I cleaned you up.'

The duck certainly looked splendid now! The doll had rubbed off all the dirt and dust, and his back shone blue, green and red. He was a fine sight to see. But what was the use of that if he had to go back to his dark shelf again! It was too bad.

'If only this rain would stop!' said the doll, squeezing the water out of her overall. 'I am always wet and always cold now. Atishoo! Atishoo!'

'Oh, don't get a cold!' begged the duck in alarm. 'If you have to go to bed, what will become of me? The policeman will turn me out, I am sure.'

'Atishoo!' sneezed the little doll. 'Oh, dear, I can't stop sneezing. Atishoo!'

Well, that very night the doll was put to bed in the farmhouse by the farmer's wife, for she really had a shocking cold. The duck swam sadly by himself on the pond, keeping a lookout in case the policeman came along. And, sure enough, he did! The duck saw him wading across the field to the pond, looking as black as thunder because he was getting so wet and muddy.

'Haven't you got some work to do yet?' he shouted to the frightened duck. 'You great lazy thing! Here you are all day long, floating about doing nothing! You can leave Toytown on Saturday! Do you hear me?'

'Yes,' said the duck unhappily.

The policeman waded off, wishing that the rain would stop. But it didn't. It went on and on and on, and soon the duck pond was so big that the duck could take a really good swim. The whole field was under water, and all the hens fled to their house at the end of the meadow, while the pigs and goats stood huddled together near the farmhouse.

I suppose the doll is in bed, thought the duck. *Poor thing! She will be sad when she knows I must leave her. I will try to see her before I go on Saturday. Perhaps she will be up by then.*

Each day the duck looked out for the doll to come, but she didn't appear. She was still in bed. The rain went on pouring down, and soon people began to say that there would be floods in Toytown. Such a thing had never happened before!

The river overflowed and joined the pond on which the duck swam. Then what a great stretch of water there was for the duck to swim on! The water spread right up to the farmhouse, and the farmer's wife rushed upstairs in fright, for it poured in at her kitchen door!

'We shall have to live in the bedrooms!' she cried. 'Oh, dear, oh, dear! What a dreadful thing! All my kitchen chairs are floating about!'

The duck knew that it was Saturday, and he thought he would swim up to the farmhouse and look in at the bedroom windows until he found the room where his friend the doll lay. Then he would say goodbye. So up he swam.

The floods were very bad now, and the water was right up to the bedroom windows! The duck swam round the farmhouse, peeping in at each window.

Then he found the doll, sitting up in bed, looking very miserable and unhappy. The duck pecked on the glass with his beak, and the little doll jumped out of bed at once.

'Oh, duck, I'm so glad you've come!' she said. 'We are in a dreadful fix here. The farmer's wife hasn't any tea, or sugar, or bread, and we don't know how to get it, because of the floods. We can't go out, for the water is right over our heads! Do you think you could float off to the butcher's and get some meat for us, and go to the grocer's and get some tea and sugar?'

'Of course!' said the duck in delight. 'I'll do

anything I can! You know that, doll! I'll go now!'

So off he floated at top speed. He went into Toytown, which was also flooded, though not quite so badly as the houses just outside. He swam to the butcher's, grocer's, baker's and milkman, and asked them for meat, tea, sugar, bread and milk, and loaded everything on to his big broad back! Then back he swam very carefully.

On the way he passed many other flooded houses. There were people at the windows, looking very miserable. When they saw the duck going by with all the parcels on his back, they began to shout excitedly to one another.

'See! There's a duck with groceries! Hie, duck! Will you get some for me? Ho there, duck! When next you go to the butcher's buy some chops for me! I say, duck, I'll give you sixpence if you'll go and fetch me some nice fresh fish from the fishmonger's.'

The duck listened to all the shouts and calls, and a marvellous idea came into his head! He would do all the shopping for the people in the flooded houses! What fun! That would really be hard work, and he would be so pleased to do it. He called out that he would soon be back, and then he floated at top speed to the farmhouse. He tapped on the window, and the doll opened it. She cried out in delight when she saw how well the duck had done the shopping. She lifted in the parcels, and as she took them the duck quacked out to her all the news.

'The houses nearby are all flooded too,' he said. 'The people want me to go and do their shopping for them. If I go and do it, doll, I shall earn money, and then that policeman can't turn me out!'

'Oh, splendid!' cried the doll. 'Tomorrow I will come with you. My cold is nearly better. I will ask the people to give me written shopping lists, and then we will go together and buy everything.'

So the next day the doll sat on the duck's back, and he swam with her round to all the flooded houses. Everyone handed her a shopping list, and the duck and the doll hurried to the shops to get what was wanted. Then, when the duck's back was quite loaded, back they floated to the houses and handed in the goods at the windows. They were paid sixpence each time they went shopping, and soon the little bag that the doll kept the money in jingled and clinked as she shopped. What a lot of money they were making!

'I shall be quite sorry when the rain stops,' said the little doll. She had bought herself a mackintosh and sou'wester, and also a pair of Wellington boots. So she was quite all right. Everyone looked out for the little couple each morning now, and called to them from the top windows.

One day, when the doll and duck were floating past the police station on their way to the shops, a window was flung open, and the toy policeman called to them.

'Hie!' he said. 'Come here!'

'Oh, dear! Do you suppose he wants to turn me out now?' said the poor duck, trembling so much that the doll was nearly shaken off his back. 'I shan't go to him. I shall just pretend I don't see him.'

'Oh, we'd better go,' said the doll. 'It isn't good to be cowardly. Let's be brave and go.'

So they floated across to him. To their great surprise he beamed at them, and said, 'Well, you certainly have made yourselves useful, you two! Now look, here is my shopping list. Will you do my shopping for me too? I cannot get out of the police station.'

So they went to do the policeman's shopping as well, and weren't they pleased to put sixpence into their bag!

In three weeks' time the rain stopped and the floods began to go down. Little by little all the water drained away, and people were able to go in and out of the doors of their houses. The field round the farmhouse dried up and the little pond was itself again. The farmer came to the gate and called to the doll.

'What about coming back to be my gardener again?' he shouted. 'The duck can have the use of my pond, if he wishes!'

'Oh, dear!' groaned the duck. 'What a dull life that will be, after these exciting three weeks!'

'Don't worry, duck,' said the doll, hugging him hard round the neck. 'I've got such a lovely idea!'

The duck was on the river, and the doll stepped off and ran to the farmer. 'I'm sorry I can't come back,' she said, 'but I've bought a little house by the river, and the duck and I are going to live there, and do all the fetching and carrying for the folk who live on the riverside!'

The duck nearly fell over on the water when he heard this. Live with the doll in a little house – and work for her! Oh, could anything be better?

It was quite true. The doll had spent her money well. She swam off with the duck and took him to a tiny house on the riverside. It had curtains at the windows, and a tiny landing stage.

'There you are!' she said. 'That's our house! And all the folk who live nearby have promised that they will call you whenever they want to be taken from one side of the river to the other, duck – and if they want any shopping done, we can go and get their shopping lists, and you can float with me down the river, until we come to the town. Then I shall jump off and do the shopping, and you can wait for me. I'll come back and put the parcels on your back, and off we'll go up the river once more. Isn't that lovely!'

So that's what they do now. And in the evening, when the work is done, the doll carries the duck into her little house, and they sit on chairs opposite one another and drink hot cocoa together.

Ah, they have a fine life together! But they did work hard for it, didn't they?

A Tale of Shuffle, Trot and Merry

A Tale of Shuffle, Trot and Merry

'NOW COME along!' shouted Mr Smarty. 'Where are you, Shuffle, Trot and Merry? I've some shopping here ready for you to take to my house!'

They were playing marbles in a corner of the market. Shuffle groaned. 'Blow! Now we've got to put his sacks of shopping on our backs and walk for miles to his house. I'm tired of it! Why doesn't he buy a horse and cart for us to drive?'

'Because it's too expensive,' said Trot. 'Come along – he'll be cross if we don't hurry.'

They went over to Mr Smarty, who was standing by three big sacks.

'Oh, so there you are, you lazy lot!' he said. 'I've bought all these things at the market, and I want them taken to my house as quickly as possible.'

'It's too hot to walk fast with big sacks like those!' said Shuffle.

'We won't get there before midnight,' said Trot gloomily.

'Well, I'll do my best,' said Merry.

'I'll give a gold piece to the one who gets to my house first,' said Mr Smarty.

They pricked up their ears at that! A gold piece! That was riches to them.

Sly old Shuffle went over to the sacks at once, and quickly felt them all. Oh, what a heavy one, and the second was heavy too, but the third one felt as light as a feather! That was the one for him!

I shall hardly know I've a sack on my back! he thought. *I'll easily be the first one there and I'll get the gold piece!*

He shuffled off with the very light sack on his back.

Trot went over to the two sacks left, wondering what was in them.

He stuck a finger into one. It was full of something round and hard – potatoes, perhaps? He stuck a finger into the other and felt something loose and soft. What was it – flour, salt, sugar? He pulled out his finger and sucked it. It tasted sweet and delicious.

'Ah – sugar!' he said. 'Lovely! I can cut a tiny hole in the sack and dip my finger into the sugar all the time I'm walking along. What a treat!'

So Trot took the second sack and set off to catch up with Shuffle. Merry whistled a happy tune and went to the sack that was left. He made a face as he lifted it on to his back.

'It's heavy – full of potatoes, I think – probably covered in mud too, which makes them twice as heavy. Well, here goes, I must catch up Shuffle and Trot before they get too far, or I won't win that gold piece!'

But it was difficult to catch up with Shuffle, even though he was not the fastest walker as a rule, because his sack was so very, very light. Shuffle had no idea what was inside, and he didn't care. He was delighted to have picked such a light load!

That gold piece is as good as in my pocket! he thought. *And I'm going to keep it all for myself!*

Trot was having quite a good time with his sack, as he trotted along eating the sugar. *What a joke*, he thought – he was lightening his load and having a feast at the same time!

Merry walked fast, but his load was really heavy – and then he had the bad luck to stub his toe on a big stone, and that made him limp!

'Just my luck!' he groaned. 'I'll never catch up with the others now. I can't walk fast with a sore toe!'

So Merry fell behind, but all the same he whistled a merry tune and smiled at anyone he passed. But soon clouds began to cover the sun, and a wind blew up and made the trees sway to and fro. Then Merry felt a drop of rain on his face and he sighed.

'Now it's going to pour with rain and I shall

get soaked. I'd better give up all hope of getting that gold piece!'

The rain began to pelt down, stinging the faces of the three little fellows. Shuffle was a great way ahead of the others, and he grinned as he looked round and saw how far behind they were.

But, as the rain poured down, odd things began to happen! First of all, Shuffle's sack grew heavier!

Is my sack getting heavy, or am I just imagining it? he thought.

He walked a little further and then felt that he must have a rest. 'My sack feels twice as heavy! Whatever can be inside?' He set it down and untied the rope. He put in his hand and felt something soft, squashy and wet! The rain had gone right into the sack. Can you guess what it was inside?

It was a sponge! 'No wonder the sack felt so light when the sponges were dry!' said Shuffle in dismay. 'Now they're soaked with rain and as heavy as can be! What can I do?'

Trot came along, grinning. 'Hallo, Shuffle. So your load was sponges, was it? It serves you right for picking the lightest load as usual. Now you've got the heaviest!'

'What's in your sack?' called Shuffle, annoyed, but Trot didn't stop. No, he saw a chance of winning that gold piece now. He was going quite fast. Also his sack felt lighter!

In fact, it soon felt so light that Trot stopped in surprise. *What's happening?* he thought. *My sack feels remarkably light!*

He put it down to see – and, to his horror, he found that the sugar was melting in the rain and dropping fast out of the bottom of the sack!

I ought to get under cover, or it will all be melted away, thought Trot in dismay. *Why didn't I remember that sugar melts? Well, I've outpaced old Shuffle – but if I wait till the rain stops, Merry will be sure to catch me up and pass me, and I shan't get the gold piece.*

So on he went in the pouring rain, while the sugar

in his sack melted faster than ever. But at least he was now in the lead!

As for Merry he still whistled in the pouring rain, for he was a lighthearted fellow. The rain ran into his sack, down among the potatoes, and soon muddy water was dripping out at the bottom. Merry laughed.

'You're washing all the dirty potatoes for me!' he said to the rain clouds above. 'Hallo, there's Shuffle in front of me. He's very slow today!'

He soon passed Shuffle, who groaned loudly as Merry passed him. 'My load is sponges!' he shouted. 'And they're four times as heavy as they were, now that they're soaked with rain.'

'Serves you right!' said Merry. 'You picked the lightest sack so that you could win that gold piece!'

The three went on through the rain, and at last came one by one to Mr Smarty's big house. Trot arrived at the back door first and set down his sack on the ground.

'Hallo!' said the cook. 'Have you brought

something for the master? I'll tell him you were the first to arrive.'

The next was Merry with his sack of potatoes. The cook peered at them and smiled. 'Well I never – the potatoes are all washed clean for me! That's a good mark for you, Merry.'

Last of all came poor Shuffle, very weary with carrying such a wet and heavy load. He set his sack down and water from the sponges ran all over the floor.

'Now pick up that sack and stand it outside!' said the cook. 'My floor's in enough mess already without you making it a running river. What in the world have you got in that sack?'

But Shuffle was too tired to answer. The cook gave them all some food and drink and they sat back and waited to be seen by Mr Smarty.

At last they were sent for, and the cook took them into his study.

'Here's the one who arrived first,' she said, pushing Trot forward. His sack looked limp, wet and empty.

Mr Smarty glared at it in rage.

'What's this? It should be full of sugar! Where's the sugar, Trot? Have you sold it to someone on the way?'

'No, sir. The rain melted it,' said Trot. 'I was here first, sir. Can I have my gold piece?'

'Bah! You don't deserve it,' said Mr Smarty. 'Why didn't you get under cover and save my expensive sugar?' Then he turned to Shuffle.

'Shuffle, you were third, so you're out of it. Take that disgusting, dripping sack out of the room. Merry, what about you?'

'Sir, he's brought potatoes – and they're all washed clean!' said the cook eagerly, for she liked Merry. 'He deserves the gold piece, even though he wasn't the first here!'

Merry laughed. 'The rain did the cleaning!' he said.

'You weren't the first,' said Mr Smarty, 'but you certainly delivered my goods in a better condition than when I bought them – so I shall award the gold piece for that.' He tossed a shining coin to the delighted Merry, who went happily off to the kitchen. What sulks and grumbles met him from Shuffle and Trot!

He clapped them on the shoulder.

'Cheer up – we'll go and spend my gold piece together. What's good luck for but to be shared?'

They all went out arm in arm and the cook stared after them, smiling.

'You deserve good luck, Merry!' she called. 'And you'll always get it – a merry face and a generous heart are the luckiest things in the world!'

I think she could be right.

Mr Big-Hat's Button

Mr Big-Hat's Button

'DAME PIPPY, I want you to turn out my big cupboard,' said Mr Big-Hat the wizard.

'Yes, Mr Big-Hat,' said Dame Pippy. She came in to work for the wizard every day. She was a little bit afraid of him because he knew such powerful magic. When he was making spells she always locked herself away in the kitchen.

'You never know when he's going to use thunder and lightning in his spells, or a dozen black cats,' she said to her friends. 'And, my! What a temper he's got! I never dare to peep into any of his books, or even so much as open his desk!'

'I should think not, Dame Pippy!' said Mother Woolly, her friend. 'That wouldn't be very honest. It never does to peep and pry, or to take even the smallest thing that belongs to anyone else!'

'As if I would!' said Dame Pippy crossly. 'My word, I'm scared even to dust with all the magic about that place!'

When she turned out Mr Big-Hat's cupboard Dame Pippy found a lot of interesting things. There were big old books of forgotten spells. There were bottles of strange-smelling liquids that changed colour as she looked at them. There were boxes of strange powders that made her sneeze if she opened them.

My word! There must be a lot of old magic about this cupboard! thought Dame Pippy. *And isn't it dusty? Now what's in this tin that rattles so?*

She cautiously opened the tin. Inside was a collection of buttons. You should have seen them!

There were all sizes and shapes and colours – red

and blue and green and yellow, round and square and oblong, big and small.

'The pretty things!' said Dame Pippy, and she ran her fingers through them. 'I'd like to have these buttons in my workbasket! That's where they ought to be, not in this dusty old cupboard, where no one will ever see them or use them.'

But she didn't dare to take the tin of buttons and put it into her workbasket. Dear me! Mr Big-Hat might fly into one of his dreadful tempers if she did such a thing as that!

She was just shutting down the lid when she saw a very bright red button, perfectly round, with five little holes in the middle of it. She looked at it.

Now I do believe that would match the missing button on my husband's red dressing gown, she thought. *Yes, I do believe it would!*

She took it out and put it back again. Then she took it out again. *Mr Big-Hat would never miss a little red button like that*, she thought to herself. *Why, I don't suppose he even knows there's a whole* tin *of buttons here. It would be silly of me not to take this little button now I've seen it. I'm sure it would match perfectly, and it's just the right size.*

Without thinking any more about it Dame Pippy took the round red button from the tin and slipped it into her apron pocket. Then she shut the tin, put it back on the shelf and went on cleaning out the cupboard.

When she got home that night she took out her husband's dressing gown and put the little red button against the other buttons. But, alas, it didn't match at all! It wasn't a bit the same colour. Bother!

She put it on the table and left it there. Soon Mother Woolly came in for a chat and she saw the button there. 'My! Do you want that?' she said. 'I believe it would just match the buttons on the jersey of the little boy next door. He's lost one.'

'Well, take it,' said Dame Pippy, though she knew quite well she had no right to say that at all! It wasn't hers to give – and it hadn't been hers to take either!

Mother Woolly stayed for a while and then went home, taking the button with her. Dame Pippy forgot all about it until the next day. Then she got a horrid shock.

'When you turned out that cupboard of mine, did you happen to see a tin of buttons?' asked Mr Big-Hat.

Dame Pippy went red. 'Y-y-yes, sir,' she said.

'Good!' said Mr Big-Hat. 'I hoped they would be there. Get the tin for me, Dame Pippy. I want a special button out of it.'

Dame Pippy went to get the tin. Oh my goodness! How she hoped it wouldn't be that silly little red button that Mr Big-Hat wanted!

He took the tin from her and emptied all the buttons on to his table. 'It's a scarlet button,' he said. 'Quite round. With five little holes in the middle. A very, very special button for use in a very powerful spell. It's a button off the dress of one of the cleverest witches that ever lived. Must be chock-full of magic. Now, where is it?'

Dame Pippy couldn't say a word. Her knees shook. That button! She knew it wasn't there. She had given it to Mother Woolly. Oh, why, why had she been so foolish as to take it?

'Strange!' said Mr Big-Hat in a cross voice. 'It doesn't seem to be here. Dame Pippy, it must have rolled out into the cupboard. Will you please go and look – and go *on* looking in that cupboard till you find it. It is *most important*.'

'Y-y-y-y-yes, sir,' stammered poor Dame Pippy.

She went off to the room where the cupboard stood. What was the use of looking? She knew the button wasn't there. But she dared not tell the wizard. No, no, she'd rather run away and never come back!

Dame Pippy slipped out of the back door, still trembling. She saw that the smoke from Mr Big-Hat's chimney had suddenly turned yellow. That meant he was making a very powerful spell indeed – a spell that might want that button! She must be quick!

She banged on Mother Woolly's door. 'Did you give that red button to the little boy next door?' she cried. 'I want it back!'

'Yes, I gave it to his mother,' said Mother Woolly. 'Why?'

But Dame Pippy did not wait to answer. She ran next door and banged on the door there. *Funny!* thought Mother Woolly. *She's come out without her coat or hat and in her old working slippers. And it's raining!*

'Could I have that red button Mother Woolly gave you?' begged Dame Pippy when the woman of the house came to the door. 'Did you put it on your boy's jersey?'

'No. It didn't match,' said the woman. 'I gave it to John to play with. Johnny, what did you do with that button?'

'I gave it to my cousin Ella,' said John. 'She said she had lost one of her red tiddlywinks, so I thought the button would do instead. She lives up the hill, Dame Pippy.'

'Oh, dear!' said Dame Pippy, and tore up the hill in the rain, her hair getting wetter and wetter. She came to the house of Johnny's cousin Ella and banged on the door.

'*Have* you got that red button that John gave Ella?' she asked. 'I need it back. It's most important.'

'Oh, Ella was playing tiddlywinks with it when Too-Tall came in,' said Ella's mother. 'And he said he would like to have the button to sew on a red belt he has – it was just the right size. I gave it to him.'

'Oh, *my*!' said poor Dame Pippy. 'Mr Too-Tall lives miles away – and it's pouring with rain. Why didn't I bring an umbrella?'

Off she went again, her shoes quite soaked through, her breath coming in pants and puffs. Mr Too-Tall lived in the woods. Dame Pippy got there at last and asked Mr Too-Tall to please, please give her back the red button.

'Well, I sewed it on a red belt I had and gave it to my sister Katie,' said Too-Tall. 'I've no doubt she will give it to you if you ask her. How wet you are! Wait a minute and I'll lend you an umbrella.'

But Dame Pippy couldn't wait. She rushed off again to Mr Too-Tall's sister Katie.

But she had gone to a work meeting, so Dame Pippy had to toil all the way across the fields to Mrs Busy's house, where the working meeting was being held.

'Bless us all! How wet you are!' said Mrs Busy. 'And look at your shoes! Come in and tell me what you want.'

Dame Pippy panted out what she had come for. She looked for the belt on Katie's waist. But it wasn't there.

'I'm so sorry, but the red button came off the belt while I was walking here,' said Katie. 'Too-Tall didn't sew it on properly. So off came the button and down dropped my belt. I picked up the belt – but I couldn't find the button. It dropped somewhere by the stile.'

Almost crying now with the wet and the cold, poor Dame Pippy stumbled off to the stile to look for the dropped button. And after she had gone down on her hands and knees and crawled about in nettles and grass and other weeds for half an hour, she actually found the scarlet button.

Tears of relief ran down her cheeks. She had got it at last. She ran all the way back to Mr Big-Hat's, hoping that he hadn't yet finished his spell.

But he had. The chimney smoke was no longer yellow. Mr Big-Hat was standing with his finger on the bell in his workroom, ringing and ringing for Dame Pippy. Why didn't she come? It was long past his dinnertime. He was hungry.

Where was Dame Pippy?

R-r-r-r-r-r-ring! went the bell as Dame Pippy staggered in through the back door. She ran straight to Mr Big-Hat's workroom, panting, her hair dripping wet and her clothes soaking.

'Oh, sir! I've been looking for that button!' she said.

'And I've got it!'

She held out her hand with the scarlet button lying in the palm. But Mr Big-Hat didn't take it.

'I made a mistake,' he said. 'It wasn't that red button I needed after all. It was a blue one. I don't want that red one. There's no magic in it.'

Well! After all she'd done, to think it was the wrong button! Dame Pippy threw her wet apron over her head and sobbed loudly. Mr Big-Hat was astonished. He saw how wet Dame Pippy was. What *had* she been doing?

'I've been all over the place for that red button,' sobbed Dame Pippy. 'And now you don't want it.'

'But why did you go all over the place?' asked Mr Big-Hat, even more astonished. 'It was in the cupboard surely?'

'It wasn't. I wanted a red button to match one missing from my husband's dressing gown,' sobbed Dame Pippy. 'And I took *your* red button. It *would* be the one you asked for! And then you didn't want it after all. Atishoo! Atishoo!'

'You have caught a dreadful cold,' said Mr Big-Hat. 'Oh, Dame Pippy, it would have been so much better to have confessed that you had taken the button when I asked you for it this morning!'

'It would have been better not to have taken it at all!' said Dame Pippy, tears pouring down her cheeks. 'Now you'll tell me to go. Now I shan't be able to work for you any more. Nobody will let me work for them. I shall lose all my friends. How dreadful for such big things to happen to me because of one tiny red button!'

'Yes, Dame Pippy – it's surprising how often big sorrows come out of small sins,' said Mr Big-Hat sadly. 'But cheer up – this time the big things are not going to happen. You have punished yourself enough, without my punishing you too. Go and get some dry things on – and some dinner for us – and I'll make a fine big spell to stop you having a very bad cold!'

Well, dear me, Dame Pippy suddenly felt much

better after that. She rushed out to get some dinner for poor, hungry Mr Big-Hat. She'd been silly and wrong and not very honest – but she'd be better now. She'd never so much as take a pin. Then Mr Big-Hat made her a spell to cure a bad cold – and he put into it the red button, which turned out to have some quite good magic in it. So, as Mr Big-Hat said, it was a good thing Dame Pippy found it after all!

Umbrella Weather

Umbrella Weather

'EILEEN DEAR, if you are going out this morning, do take an umbrella with you!' called Mother. 'It's April, you know – and we shall get some very sudden showers.'

'All right, Mummy,' said Eileen. 'I'm taking my best doll, Rosebud, for a walk, so I'll let her take her umbrella too! She's never used it yet!'

Off they went – and it wasn't very long before a big cloud blew over the sun, and then down came the April rain! Eileen only just had time to put up her umbrella. She stood her doll Rosebud beside a bush, and put up her tiny umbrella for her too.

The rain poured down, pattering on all the leaves and making them bounce up and down. The wind blew suddenly, and Eileen lost her umbrella! It was jerked out of her hand and away it went.

She ran after it and caught it just as it blew into a bush. When she went back to Rosebud, the doll was soaking wet! Her little umbrella had blown away too.

'Oh, Rosebud – how wet you are!' said Eileen. 'Where's your umbrella, your dear little red umbrella?'

She looked and looked for it, but she never saw it again. It had blown round the bush and down a rabbit hole!

A small rabbit sitting a little way down the hole was most surprised to see it coming towards him. He jumped backwards – and then he saw what it was.

'An umbrella! The thing that boys and girls use to keep off the rain. Well, how surprising that one should come down my hole.'

He was very pleased. *Now I shall be able to use it in the rain*, he thought. *How the other rabbits will envy me!*

They were all astonished to see the little rabbit with his umbrella. He didn't know how to close it, so he had to have it up all the time, even when the sun shone.

Not far away from his hole was a fine clump of primroses. The rabbit had been watching the big rosette of leaves growing, and now there were a number of yellow buds peeping up from the very middle of the leaves.

Those buds will get soaked when these sudden rainstorms come, thought the rabbit. *The rain will run right down the stems and spoil the growing buds and the opening flowers. I'll lend the plant my umbrella the very next time it rains!*

He watched for the next big cloud to blow up over the sun. When the hill suddenly darkened around him he knew that soon the rain would pour down from the sky.

Pitter-patter – the rain sounded just like tiny footsteps running everywhere. Pitter-patter!

'I'll take my umbrella over to the primroses now,'

said the little rabbit. He carefully pushed the open umbrella up the hole in front of him, and came out into the rain.

He held the little red umbrella proudly over his head and went to the primrose plant.

'You are getting very wet,' he said politely. 'Would you like to share my umbrella? It's no trouble to hold it over your buds and leaves. The rain will run down and spoil your new flowers.'

'Please don't worry about me,' said the primrose. 'It's a nice idea of yours – but if you look carefully at me you will see I really don't need an umbrella! In fact, I could lend *you* one!'

'What do you mean?' asked the rabbit, surprised. 'You haven't an umbrella, I'm sure you haven't!'

'No, not one like yours,' said the primrose. 'Just you look hard at my leaves, rabbit. Do you notice anything peculiar about them?'

'Well, they're a nice green, but that's not peculiar,' said the rabbit. 'They're very wrinkled, of course.

Very, *very* wrinkled. As wrinkled as my old grandma's furry forehead! You must be as old as she is, primrose!'

'I'm not,' said the primrose. 'I'm only about three years old – but I'm very wise, little rabbit! As wise as all primroses are in rainy weather. Those wrinkles in my leaves are as good as your umbrella!'

The rabbit looked at them. 'Dear me, yes – I see what you mean!' he said. 'When the raindrops fall on your leaves, primrose, they all run into your wrinkles – and off goes the water down the little channels!'

'Quite right!' said the primrose. 'And if you look, you'll see that I am clever enough to turn all my leaves outwards and downwards, away from my middle, where I keep my precious buds – see how the rain runs down all my wrinkles and disappears into the grass around me.'

'You are certainly very clever,' said the rabbit. 'You turn all your leaves into green wrinkled umbrellas! Why, that's a much better idea than having to carry an umbrella about all the time!'

'Well, *you* try growing wrinkled leaves then,' said the primrose, and that made the rabbit laugh. Whatever would he look like if he grew leaves?

'Here comes a tiny elf,' he said to the primrose. 'What does she want?'

'Watch,' said the primrose, and he watched. The elf broke off a wrinkled primrose leaf and ran away with it held over her head. It kept off the rain beautifully, of course.

'It really is a very good idea,' said the rabbit. And he's right – it certainly is!

Mr Meddle's Umbrella

Mr Meddle's Umbrella

WHEN MR Meddle went to stay with his Aunt Jemima she was very strict with him. She made him put on galoshes when it was wet, and a hat when it was sunny, and a scarf round his throat when the wind was cold.

'I wish you wouldn't fuss!' Meddle kept saying. 'Aunt Jemima, I wish you wouldn't FUSS!'

'Meddle, you are so silly that I'm sure I don't know what would happen to you if I didn't fuss,' said his aunt. 'I am *not* going to have you in bed with colds while you are staying here – so I am going to fuss all I like, and you will have to do as you are told.'

Now if there was one thing more than any other that Meddle hated, it was taking an umbrella out with him. He simply couldn't bear it.

'If I have to carry an umbrella, it's a perfect nuisance!' he said. 'It gets between my ankles and trips me up. It digs itself into people as I pass them, and they get angry with me. I just can't bear an umbrella.'

'Well, my dear Meddle, you'll have to take one this afternoon when you go out, because it's simply pouring with rain!' said his aunt firmly. 'Look at it – raining cats and dogs.'

'I wish it really *would* pour cats and dogs,' said Meddle. 'I've always wanted to see that, and I never have. I shan't go out this afternoon, Aunt Jemima, if you make me take an umbrella.'

'Very well,' said his aunt. 'Then you can't call at the bookshop and get your *Sunny Stories*.'

'Oh, I simply *must* have that,' said Meddle. 'Why, I might be in the book this week.'

Well, it was still raining that afternoon when

Meddle put his coat on, and told Aunt Jemima he was going out. His aunt went to the hallstand and fetched her umbrella. It was a fat red one, and had a bright red crooked handle. She gave it to him.

'You'll get wet through, if you don't take this,' she said. 'Go along now. Hurry up!'

'Bother!' said Meddle. 'Bother, bother, bother. I do so hate umbrellas.'

'Meddle, if you don't take it, you don't go out!' said Aunt Jemima. So Meddle took it, and went down the garden path. He began thinking about a story he was going to write. It was to be about a soldier who was very brave.

'He shall have a sword,' said Meddle to himself. 'An enormous sword. And he will use it like this — slash, slash, poke, poke, slash, slash!'

Meddle began to slash about with the umbrella as if it were a sword. My, he did feel grand. People stared at him in surprise as they passed, but Meddle didn't even see them.

'My soldier shall fight well!' he cried. 'Slash, slash!' He nearly knocked old Mrs Jink's hat off her head, and she scurried away in fright.

Meddle went all the way to the bookshop in the pouring rain, pretending that the umbrella was a sword. He didn't even put it up. He soon was quite soaked, and the rain dripped down his neck.

So, of course, when he got home again his coat was dripping and his hair was so wet that it looked dreadful.

'Meddle! Didn't you put up your umbrella?' cried his aunt angrily. 'Oh, you silly creature! What's the use of taking out an umbrella if you don't put it up? Now you will get a dreadful cold.'

'Atishoo!' said Meddle, with a sneeze. And the next day he was in bed, feeling very bad.

Well, when he was up and wanted to go out for a walk his Aunt Jemima looked up at the sky. 'Meddle,' she said, 'it looks like rain. I don't think I can trust you to go out. You'll only get wet again.'

'Aunt Jemima, if only you'll let me go out and buy a bottle of boiled sweets, I promise I'll take an umbrella,' said Meddle.

'But will you put it up?' asked his aunt. 'You took an umbrella last time, but you didn't put it up. And what's the use of that? Last time you said your umbrella was a sword. This time you may pretend it's a lamppost or something.'

Well, Meddle got his way. He took the fat red umbrella out of the hallstand and went off. It wasn't raining, but after a little some drops began to fall. Meddle was busy putting his hand into the bag to get out a nice red sweet, and he was cross.

'Stupid rain!' he said. 'Well, I promised my aunt to put up the umbrella, so I must.'

Meddle held his umbrella above his head, but he didn't put it up! He just held it up like a stick, without opening the umbrella at all. He was so busy with his sweets that he forgot that an umbrella must be opened when it is held up. So there he was, going down the road, getting wetter and wetter, his umbrella held unopened above his head.

'Well, well,' said Meddle to himself. 'What's the use of an umbrella, after all, I'd like to know? I'm getting just as wet as if I'd not taken one with me at all. Splash, splash, splash, the rain comes down – and I'm getting soaked.'

Now Aunt Jemima was watching for Meddle when he came home – and when she saw him walking up the path with his umbrella held like a stick over his head she was really very angry. Meddle saw her frowning and he was puzzled.

'Now what's the matter, Aunt?' he cried, as he walked up the path and saw her looking out of the window. 'I took the umbrella, didn't I? And I put it up, didn't I? But what's the use – I'm just as wet as ever!'

'My dear Meddle, you might as well take a pea stick to hold over your head as an umbrella, if you don't bother to put it up,' said his aunt. 'Look up and see your umbrella.'

So Meddle looked up, and saw that he had forgotten to open the umbrella, and he felt rather foolish. 'Dear me,' he said. 'I've been rather silly.'

'You'll have a cold tomorrow,' said Aunt Jemima.

'Atishoo!' said Meddle. And, of course, he was in bed with a cold the very next day.

Well, well. Aunt Jemima was very cross and not a bit nice to Meddle. When he was up again she spoke to him very sternly.

'Meddle, every time you go out in future you will take an umbrella with you,' she said. 'And you will practise putting it up and down, up and down, before you go out. Then perhaps you will remember that an umbrella is meant to be opened when it is in use.'

So Meddle practised putting the umbrella up and down, and opened and shut it a dozen times before he went out. The cat hated it. It was a great shock to her whenever Meddle suddenly opened the umbrella just in front of her.

When Meddle's cold was well enough for him to

go out his aunt made him take the umbrella with him.

'But it isn't raining!' said Meddle. 'No, Aunt, I'd look silly!'

'You'll look a lot sillier if you get a third cold, and miss your birthday party,' said Aunt Jemima. 'Take the umbrella, and don't make a fuss, Meddle.'

So Meddle took it with him, though the sun was shining brightly. He went to visit his friend Gobo, and he sat and talked to him for a long time. And, of course, when he left to go home he quite forgot to take the umbrella with him. He left it behind in Gobo's hallstand!

And when he was almost home the rain came down. How it poured! You should have seen it. Meddle got quite a shock when he felt the big raindrops stinging his face.

'Ha! Good thing I took an umbrella with me!' he said. 'A very good thing indeed. I'll put it up.'

But the umbrella wasn't there to put up. Meddle stared all around as if he thought the umbrella would come walking up. But of course it didn't.

'Bother!' said Meddle. 'Where's it gone? I know I had it when I left home. How can I put an umbrella up if it isn't here? My goodness! What will Aunt Jemima say when she sees me coming home in the rain without the umbrella? I wonder if she's looking out of the window. I won't peep and see in case she is. I'll run all the way back to Gobo's and see if I've left the umbrella there!'

If only Meddle had looked, he would have seen his aunt knocking at the window to tell him to run quickly up the garden path and come in out of the rain! Instead of that, he ran down the road again, and went all the way back to Gobo's with the rain pouring down on him. How wet he got! He dripped like a piece of seaweed.

By the time he got to Gobo's he was wet through and shivering. He banged at the door. Gobo opened it.

'I've come back for my umbrella before I get wet,' said Meddle.

'You silly! You're soaked already,' said Gobo. 'As for your umbrella I've sent Mrs Gobo to your aunt's with it. You must have missed her. I can't lend you one because I haven't got one at the moment. My goodness, won't you get wet!'

So Meddle had to run back in the rain without an umbrella at all, and his shoes went squelch, squelch, squelch, and his coat went drip, drip, drip.

How angry his Aunt Jemima was when he came in. 'Meddle! I send you out with an umbrella, and you come home in the pouring rain without it, and I knock at the window to tell you to come in and you run off down the road again, and then Mrs Gobo comes in with your umbrella, and you come home again as wet as a sponge. You'll get a very bad cold.'

'Atishoo!' said Meddle at once. 'Atishoo! I must go and get a hanky!'

And, of course, he was in bed with a bad cold the next day and missed his birthday party after all! Now he is packing up to go home because his aunt says she won't keep him any longer. Do you know what she gave him for a birthday present? Guess! An umbrella – and the handle is a donkey's head.

'I chose a donkey because I really thought it would suit you well,' said Aunt Jemima.

But I expect he will leave it on the bus, don't you?

The Secret Door

The Secret Door

'WE SHALL be dreadfully bored, staying with Great-Aunt Hannah,' said Dick gloomily. 'She's nice and kind, but there's absolutely nothing to do at Westroofs.'

'What's the house like?' asked Lucy. 'You've been there, Dick – Robin and I haven't.'

'Well, it's awfully old – and rather dark inside – and there's a big room called the library, which is lined from floor to ceiling with the dullest books you ever saw – and at night the ivy taps on the windowpane and makes you jump!' said Dick.

'Here we are!' said Robin, peering out of the car

window as they swung through a pair of enormous old gates. 'My goodness, it *is* an old house. Look at the ivy covering it from roof to ground.'

Aunt Hannah was waiting to welcome them. She was a dear old lady, with snow-white hair, pink cheeks and a very kind smile.

'Welcome to Westroofs!' she said. 'I do so hope you won't find it dull, my dears. But when I heard that your mother was ill I really thought it would be a kindness to her to have you here for a while.'

The three children felt sure that it would be very dull indeed at Westroofs. There were no horses to ride, no dogs to take for a walk and not even a cat with kittens to play with. Still, if only the weather was fine, they could go for walks and explore the countryside around.

But the weather wasn't fine. When they awoke the next morning the rain was pouring down, and it went on all day long. The children roamed about the house, not daring to play any exciting games in case they disturbed Aunt Hannah, who jumped at any sudden shout or stamping of feet.

The next day it was still raining, and the children felt quite desperate. 'I've never been so bored in my life,' groaned Dick. 'Whatever can we do? Let's go out in the rain.'

But Aunt Hannah was afraid they would get wet and catch cold. 'No, don't go out,' she said. 'Wouldn't you like to go and look at the books in the library? There are some that belonged to my great-grandfather when he lived at Westroofs. Very, very interesting.'

The children didn't feel as if Aunt Hannah's great-grandfather's books would be at all interesting, but they were much too polite to say so. They went into the big, dark library and switched on the middle light, for it was a very dull day.

'There must be hundreds and hundreds of books here that nobody ever reads or wants to read,' said Dick, looking at the crowded, dusty shelves. 'Here's one that I'm sure nobody has ever read – "History of Edward

Lucian, born 1762, in the parish of Elham!" Why, half the pages are still uncut. Poor Edward Lucian!'

'Lucian is our family name. Perhaps he was a great, great, great ancestor of ours,' said Robin. 'Look, here's a ladder in this corner. Whatever is it for?'

'To climb up to the topmost shelves, I should think, if anyone should ever want a book from there,' said Lucy. 'Let's put it up. We'll see what kind of books are kept on the top shelf. Do you suppose there are any storybooks at all?'

'Shouldn't think so,' said Robin, putting the ladder up by the shelves of books. 'Well, here I go. If I see anything exciting, I'll toss it down.'

Up he went. The top shelf was covered with thick grey dust. It flew into the air as Robin pulled out one or two books and made him sneeze. The sneeze made him drop a book, and it almost fell on Lucy's head.

'Look out, silly!' said Lucy as the book crashed to the floor. It fell half open, and something flew out of the pages.

'There! One of the pages has got loose,' said Lucy. 'I'll put it back in its right place.'

But when she picked it up she saw that it was not a loose page but an old, old letter, written on a half-sheet of paper in curious old-fashioned writing. She could hardly make out a word of what it said. She held it out to Dick.

'Look at this old letter,' she said. 'All the "s"s are shaped like "f"s. It's impossible to read.'

Robin came down the ladder. He too looked at the strange letter. He and Dick began to spell it out slowly.

'"Today – I went through – the Secret Door. I have hidden my new spinning top there, and the stick I cut from the hedge. William shall not have them. He knows not the way through – through – the Secret Door. He is not – not – allowed in the Sad— Sad—" What *is* this word? Oh, "*Saddle*". "He is not allowed in the Saddle Room, and knows not the Secret Panel there."'

The writing ended at that point. The three children were suddenly seized with a great excitement. They stared at one another, feeling rather breathless.

'It's not a letter – it must be part of a diary or something, kept by someone – a boy – who lived here years and years ago!'

'And he had a brother called William. And William didn't know about a secret panel in the saddle room, or about a secret door. Golly! Let's go and explore! *We* might find them!'

'Where's the saddle room? Oh, I know – it's the little room at the side of the house, near where the old stables used to be. And it's got panelling all round the walls, I remember! Quick, let's go!'

Forgetting all about putting the ladder back in its corner or the book back in its place, the children ran out of the dark library, down long passages and came to the saddle room.

It was a low, dark room, set round with squared oak panels. Even now there were two or three old saddles hanging on nails, and a crop lay on a shelf. The rest of the room contained chairs and tables turned out from other rooms. It was plainly a kind of storeroom now.

'Now which would be the secret panel?' said Dick, looking round at the walls. 'Golly, isn't this exciting? Where shall we try first? Not on that wall, because it's almost covered by that big old picture. Let's try over here by the fireplace.'

'How do we look for a secret panel, and what does it do?' asked Lucy. 'Do we press or push or what?'

'A secret panel was usually put into a wall of panelling to conceal a cupboard, or some sort of secret way out or in,' said Dick. 'We must press each one, and jiggle it, and see if we can make one move.'

Dick began to knock around on the walls. Thud, thud, thud.

'I might hear if one panel sounds hollow,' he said. 'If it did, I'd know it could be the secret one.'

But none of them sounded hollow. It was most disappointing.

'Perhaps the panel is behind that big picture after

all,' said Dick. 'Let's move it.'

But they couldn't. It was much too heavy. They gazed around the little room in despair. Then Dick went to where a saddle hung on a great nail, and took it down. 'I haven't tried *this* panel,' he said, and knocked on it. It sounded hollow!

'It must be the one!' cried Lucy, and they all pushed at the brown polished panel, and banged on it. But nothing happened. In desperation Dick caught hold of the big nail and pulled at it.

And then, before their eyes, the panel slid downwards a little, and then sideways, quite soundlessly. Behind it was a dark space. The children stared breathlessly.

'We've found it! We've found the secret panel. What's in the hole?'

Dick sped off for his torch, and soon the children were peering into the hole left by the sliding panel. There didn't seem anything to see at all – just a hole, dark and empty.

'Well, if that isn't disappointing!' said Robin. 'Just

a hole. And anyway, where's the secret door we read about? There's no door here. Nobody could get through this hole.'

Dick put his hand right into the dark hole and groped around. His hand suddenly found what seemed to be a handle or knob of some kind. He pulled it.

Behind the children came a sudden grating noise, then a terrific crash. They all jumped violently, very frightened. They looked round, scared.

'It's that big picture. It fell off the wall,' said Dick. 'And, gosh – look – there's a space behind it. It's the secret door!'

The children stared in delight. There was an opening in the panelling where the great picture had been, an opening big enough to get through! Where did it lead to?

'When I pulled that knob in the hole here it must have worked something that opened the secret door,' said Dick. 'And when it opened the picture had to fall, of course. Oh, it did make me jump!'

A deep sound suddenly boomed through the house. 'The gong – it's dinnertime!' said Lucy with a groan. 'Just as we have found this exciting secret door!'

'Better shut it up again,' said Dick. 'We won't say a word to Aunt Hannah about it until we've explored a bit. We might find family treasure or something. You never know!'

Visions of glittering jewels, bags of silver and gold and boxes of coins flashed into the minds of the children. It was very hard to pull at the knob inside the hole and see the secret door shut itself when they so badly wanted to go through it. They couldn't lift the heavy picture up again, so they left it standing against the wall. Then they went to wash their hands.

Aunt Hannah beamed at them as they took their places at the table.

'Well,' she said, 'it has stopped raining at last – and I have arranged a treat for you this afternoon.'

The children looked blank. A treat? The only treat they wanted was to go through that secret door! Why had the rain stopped? They didn't want to leave the house now.

'I've telephoned to Farthington – that's our nearest big town, you know,' said Aunt Hannah, 'and I've got tickets for the circus there, for you. A car is coming at half past two, and you shall have a late tea at a very nice shop in Farthington that has chocolate eclairs and meringues.'

Now ordinarily this would have been a simply glorious treat, but not today! Still, since everything was all arranged, the children could only say thank you and go!

'We'll have to explore this evening,' said Dick gloomily. 'I can hardly wait! What a pity the circus couldn't have been tomorrow.'

It was glorious. Aunt Hannah came too and seemed to enjoy everything very much.

'Now when we get home we will have a quiet game of cards together,' she said. 'I don't want you to get overexcited tonight, after such an exciting afternoon.'

So once again exploring had to be put off, and the children played Happy Families and Snap until bedtime. It was terribly disappointing.

Just as Lucy was about to fall asleep in her bed that night the two boys came cautiously into her room. 'Lucy! Are you awake? We're going to go through that secret door now, tonight! We simply can't wait. Do you want to come, or will you be frightened, because it's night?'

'Of *course* I want to come!' said Lucy, wide awake immediately. 'I'll put on my dressing gown at once. Oh, how super! I never, never thought you'd go tonight!'

Trembling with excitement, Lucy followed the two boys downstairs and along the passages that led to the saddle room. Dick pulled at the nail that opened the secret panel. It swung aside as before. He put in his hand and pulled at the knob behind. With a grating noise the secret door opened in the panelling nearby, and the children stared into the gaping hole.

Dick shone his torch there. 'A short passage, then steps,' he said in excitement. 'Come on!'

He climbed through the secret door, and the others followed. The passage was very short and ended at some narrow, very steep stone steps that led downwards. Dick felt hot with excitement. Where did they lead to?

He went down cautiously, afraid of falling. The others followed. There were fifteen of these steps, then they ended, and another passage came in sight.

'We must be below ground now!' said Dick. 'Here's another passage leading away from the house. I do wonder what it used to be for?'

'Oh, most old houses had secret passages or hiding places,' said Robin. 'People in olden days often needed to hide their treasure from enemies – or even to hide themselves. Goodness, isn't it dark? And the roof's so low just here that I have to bend my head.'

It was very weird walking along the narrow, musty passage so far underground. It curved about to avoid rocky parts. Then suddenly Dick came to a standstill.

'Blow! There's been a fall here! Look. The roof has fallen in and we can't get by.'

The others crowded up to him and looked over his shoulder. 'Yes, we *can* get by,' said Robin. 'We can kick away the rubble at this side, look, and make a way through. It's easy.'

They did manage to make their way through and then, covered with dust, they came to a small underground room! An old bench stood at one side, and a crock for water. On a rough shelf was a dust-covered spinning top and a strange curved stick.

The children gazed at them in delight.

'The spinning top and the stick, which that boy of long ago hid from his brother William,' said Dick at last. 'How weird. He never came to fetch them again.'

They stood in silence, looking around the bare little room – and then Robin gave an amazed cry. He bent down and picked up something. 'Look,' he said, 'do look – *a cigarette end*!'

So it was. The others could hardly believe their

eyes. 'How did it get here? Who has been here? And when?'

As they stood there they suddenly heard a noise. It seemed to come from above their heads. They looked up and saw that the roof seemed to have a hole in it.

And then, even as they looked, the end of a rope appeared, and the rope itself slid through the hole, touching Dick on the shoulder. He shut off his torch at once.

'Someone's coming! But what are they doing here? It's almost midnight. They must be up to something!'

'Get back to where that heap of rubble is,' whispered Robin. 'We can squeeze through again and stay at the other side and listen. Quick!'

With beating hearts the three hurried to the mass of rubble, squeezed through as quietly as they could, and then stood waiting in the dark, listening and peering through the cracks in the rubble that stretched from floor to roof.

Someone slid down the rope. Then a torch flashed

on. 'Come on, Bill,' said a man's voice. 'Buck up with the stuff!'

The man took a candle from his pocket, and set it on the wooden bench. He lit it, and the children saw by its flickering flame that the man in the underground room was thickset and very short. As he stood there, waiting, something fell through the hole in the roof, and the man caught it deftly. Then another package came, looking like a sack of something, and then another.

A muffled voice sounded down the hole. 'That's all, Shorty. Come on up. We'll fetch it tomorrow.'

Shorty hauled himself up the rope, after blowing out the candle. Then there was silence. The children waited for a while, then cautiously made their way back to the underground room again. There were now three sacks there, tied up at the necks.

'They're full of something hard,' said Dick, feeling them. 'Got a pocketknife on you, Robin?'

Nobody had, because they all wore dressing gowns.

Robin managed to untie one of the sacks. It was full of little jewel boxes. Lucy opened one and gasped.

Inside was a most beautiful necklace that glittered brilliantly in the light of the torch. All the other boxes contained jewellery too.

'Looks like the result of a very successful robbery!' said Dick. 'What a wonderful place to hide it! I suppose the burglars didn't know there was another way to this room besides that hole in the roof. What shall we do? Drag the sacks back to the house?'

'Oh, *yes*,' said Lucy. 'They will be such a surprise for Aunt Hannah. I'd love to see her face when she sees all these. And it would be too awful to leave them here in case those men came back and got them!'

So, puffing and panting, the children dragged a sack each through the rubble and up the passage to the stone steps. Up the steps they went, and along to the secret door. They dumped the sacks in the saddle room and sat down, panting and excited.

'You go and wake Aunt Hannah, Lucy,' said Dick.

So she went up to her great-aunt's room and knocked on the door.

'What is it?' came Aunt Hannah's startled voice. 'Oh, you, Lucy. Is somebody ill?'

'No. But, Aunt Hannah, do put on your dressing gown and come down to the saddle room,' begged Lucy.

'To the *saddle* room – in the middle of the night!' said Aunt Hannah, beginning to think it was all a dream. 'Dear, dear, whatever's happening?'

Soon she was down in the saddle room, astonished to see the sacks there, and even more astonished to see the secret door.

'Good gracious!' she said. 'So you've found that! The door has not been used for ages and has been forgotten so long that nobody ever knew where it was – except you children apparently! Well, well, well – now tell me what's been happening.'

So they told her, and when they showed her what was in the sacks Aunt Hannah could hardly believe her eyes. She gasped and blinked, and couldn't find a word to say.

'I suppose we'd better ring up the police, hadn't we?' said Dick. 'We could hand these to them and tell them about the burglars' plan to go to the underground room tomorrow night – and they could catch them beautifully!'

The police were amazed, and very pleased. 'Ho, so it was Shorty and Bill, was it?' said the inspector. 'Well, we've been wanting them for a very long time! The stolen goods all belong to the duchess of Medlington – my word, she'll be glad to have them back! Smart work, children!'

'Well, it was all because of William's brother, really,' said Lucy, and the inspector stared at her in surprise. William's brother? Whatever was the child talking about?

'Now you really must go to bed, children,' said Aunt Hannah. 'It's two o'clock in the morning. Shocking! No more finding of secret doors and underground rooms and stolen goods tonight, please.

Off to bed with you!'

'Well,' said Dick, as they got into bed at last, 'we thought this would be the dullest place in the world to stay at, but it's given us a most exciting adventure.'

So it had – and it was even more exciting when the inspector telephoned the next night to say that he had got Bill and Shorty all right. 'You can't think how astonished they were when they found that their sacks had vanished out of that hole!' chuckled the inspector. 'And they were even more amazed when my men popped down on top of them.'

'Wish I'd been there,' said Dick. 'I say, Aunt Hannah – do you think I might have that long-ago boy's spinning top? It still spins beautifully.'

'Of course,' said Aunt Hannah. 'And Robin can have the walking stick, cut so many years ago from the hedge. And, as for Lucy, she can have this tiny brooch, which has been sent to her by the duchess herself! There you are, Lucy – now none of you will ever forget the adventure of the secret room!'

The Blow-Abouts

The Blow-Abouts

IT WAS a very windy day – so windy that all the trees were bent over, and all the grasses sang a little whistling song. Mollie and John were hurrying home from school, and the wind played them all sorts of tricks as they went.

First it blew John's book away, and sent it flying along the grass. Then it took Mollie's hat right off her head. Every time Mollie bent down to pick it up the wind blew it a little further off again, and, really, it seemed exactly as if it was playing with her.

Suddenly Mollie stopped and pointed up in the air.

'Look, John!' she cried. 'Whatever's that coming down from the sky?'

John looked.

'It looks like a crowd of little people hanging on to a big toy balloon!' he said. 'What a peculiar thing!'

Sure enough, it was! The big blue balloon came quickly downwards, and hanging on to its string were four small people that looked rather like pixie folk. They rolled over and over on the ground as the balloon came to earth. Then they picked themselves up and dusted their coats.

'Here's a fine thing!' said the biggest one. 'Now what are we to do?'

'What's the matter?' asked John, running up. 'Do you always go about on the string of a balloon?'

'Yes, because we are the Blow-Abouts. Didn't you know?' said the biggest one. 'We're always blowing about somewhere. But our balloon is gradually getting smaller. Look at it – the poor thing has almost gone to nothing now. There must be a leak in it somewhere, for it was quite all right when we started out this morning.'

'Where are we?' asked the smallest Blow-About. 'I suppose this is part of Fairyland, isn't it?'

'No, it's the place where men and women and boys and girls live,' said Mollie. 'Have you come from Fairyland?'

'No, from Dreamland,' answered the Blow-About. 'We were on our way to Fairyland, you know. I suppose the wind must have blown us out of our way – it's in a very mischievous mood this morning, isn't it?'

'How are we to get back?' asked the biggest Blow-About. 'We really must get to Fairyland tonight, you know. We promised to sing at the queen's party.'

'Well, our balloon is busted,' said the littlest one.

'You shouldn't say "busted", you should say "bursted",' said the biggest one.

'But that's not right either,' said John.

'Don't argue,' said all the Blow-Abouts at once.

'Can't you advise us how to get back?'

'No,' said John, thinking hard, 'I can't. I haven't a balloon and my toy aeroplane is broken and—Oh, I know!'

'What?' cried Mollie and the Blow-Abouts together.

'There's my umbrella that blew inside out yesterday,' said John. 'Could we use that somehow, do you think?'

'The very thing!' cried the biggest Blow-About. 'We'll go with you and see it.'

So all six of them ran off together, and John fetched his broken umbrella from the playroom and showed it to the Blow-Abouts. The biggest Blow-About looked at it and frowned. Then he suddenly clapped his hands.

'I've got it!' he cried. 'We'll make a kind of parachute! Quick! Help me to take out this stick!'

Together they worked the stick of the umbrella out. They had to cut it at the end, and soon the umbrella looked very peculiar.

'Get a big curtain ring and some strong string,' commanded the biggest Blow-About, getting very hot as he worked.

Mollie found a curtain ring, and John brought some string.

'Thanks,' said the Blow-About. He cut the string into equal pieces, and tied each piece to a point of the umbrella. Then he tied all the other ends of the string to the curtain ring.

'Now there's a fine parachute!' he cried. 'All it wants is the wind to blow it along! Come along now, and maybe we'll catch the five o'clock breeze!'

'The five o'clock breeze!' cried Mollie. 'I didn't know there were winds like that!'

'You don't know much!' said the biggest Blow-About cheekily. 'You have five o'clock buses and trains and things, don't you? Well, we have winds that run to time too and take us where we want to go!'

'How are we all going to get on to the parachute?' asked the littlest Blow-About anxiously. 'There's only one curtain ring to hold on to, you know!'

'We'll manage somehow!' said the biggest one. He caught hold of the ring and held on as the wind filled the parachute and lifted it. 'Catch hold of my legs, one of you! Here comes the wind!'

One of the Blow-Abouts did so and then the next took hold of the second one's feet. The littlest one of all, who was really hardly any weight, caught hold of the third one – and then off they went into the air on the five o'clock wind!

Up they went, up and up, while Mollie and John shouted in delight.

'Thanks very much!' cried the Blow-Abouts. 'This is ever so much better than a balloon! We shall always use your old umbrella, John.'

And, as far as I know, they always have. They sometimes come blowing over our land on a moonlit night, so you must watch out for them. Mollie and John have only seen them once more, and then they noticed that their old umbrella was painted in very bright colours. So, as John said, 'It's just as well not to throw anything away because you never know when Blow-Abouts or someone like them will come along and use it!'

Melia's Moneybox

Melia's Moneybox

MELIA WAS one of five children. She was the middle
one of the five. There was nine-year-old Jack,
eight-year-old Fanny, seven-year-old Melia and the
six-year-old twins, Alice and Dick.

'I'm Melia the middle one,' Melia told visitors, and
that made them laugh. 'Melia Middle,' they said,
and kissed her because she was such a jolly, smiling
little girl.

One day Grandpa arrived with a present for
everyone. 'Moneyboxes!' he said, and he gave one to
each of his grandchildren. They were sweet. They
were like little houses and you had to put the coin in at

the wide chimneypot. Each house had the name of its owner painted on it.

'There you are!' said Grandpa, giving each child one. 'It's time you all learnt to save some of your money. You must put aside a bit for a rainy day, you know.'

'Well, I don't want to spend money on a rainy day,' said Melia. 'Mummy doesn't often let me go out when it's pouring with rain.'

That made Grandpa laugh. He told Melia that putting money away for a rainy day meant saving up in case you suddenly had to buy something you didn't expect.

'Grown-ups save money in case somebody is ill and they have to pay for doctors and medicines,' said Grandpa. 'Children should learn to save up too – they should buy birthday presents for their mothers and fathers, and things like that.'

The children liked their moneyboxes. It was fun to pop coins into the chimney and hear them fall with a crash. You could get them out by undoing a trapdoor with a key, at the very bottom of the house.

'Now,' said Grandpa, 'I am going to take you all to the zoo in a few weeks' time, and I want you to save up for it. I shall double any money you have in your moneyboxes when the time comes – so if you want carousel rides and things like that, you had better save hard. We will see who is the best at saving.'

The children began to save. 'If I save four shillings and Grandpa doubles it, I shall have eight shillings to spend at the zoo!' said Jack, and he put into the box every penny and threepence coin that anyone gave him.

Melia managed to save sixpence, and then she heard that Benny, a little friend of hers, was very ill. She was sad for him, and she unlocked her moneybox and took out five pennies. That only left a penny inside. She bought a bunch of sweet peas and took it round to Benny.

'The smell makes me feel better,' he said. 'You *are* kind, Melia.'

'You're silly,' said Jack when he heard about it. 'Now you've only got a penny left.'

But soon Melia had one shilling and one penny inside, because Auntie Rose came and gave everyone something to spend. How the moneyboxes clinked!

Then Melia's teacher at school told them about a poor old woman she knew who had no money to buy herself some spectacles. She had broken hers, and could not see to read or sew. She asked the children if they could each spare a penny to help the old woman to buy her glasses.

Melia rushed home and emptied her moneybox. She took all the money to her teacher. 'Here you are,' she said, 'give her all this. I'm so sorry for that poor old woman.'

So that meant Melia had to start all over again. Even the twins had more money in the boxes than Melia. It was silly of Melia, Jack said, to keep giving away all her money.

'Well, I really will try to save now,' said Melia.

She didn't buy any sweets. She didn't buy the doll's shoes she saw in the toyshop. She didn't buy anything at all.

Then she had almost one shilling in her box, and she felt pleased. It was hard to save up money, and give up things she wanted, but it felt nice to think she had something in her moneybox.

Then Granny fell down and broke her leg! All the children were sad, because they loved little old Granny. 'If Grandpa didn't want us to save our money, I'd buy her some flowers,' said Jack.

'He might be cross if we opened our moneyboxes so near the time when he's taking us to the zoo,' said Fanny.

'Granny's got plenty of flowers in her own garden,' said the twins, who didn't want to open their moneyboxes just when they were getting so full. 'She doesn't need any more flowers.'

Only Melia said nothing. She did love little old Granny so much. A broken leg must hurt. Perhaps

Granny would never be able to walk any more. Melia couldn't bear it.

I won't buy flowers, because they all say Granny has plenty, she thought, *but I* must *take her a present. I like presents when I'm ill. I'm sure Granny does too. Oh, dear – and I was trying so hard to save up too. But Granny's broken leg is more important than my savings!* Melia opened her moneybox and took out all the money.

'You're a naughty girl,' said Jack. 'Grandpa will be cross with you, always spending your money like that. What are you going to do with it?'

Melia didn't like to tell him. Jack would laugh at her, she felt sure. She was going to spend all her money on some special peppermints that Granny loved! Off she went and bought a whole bagful.

Granny was so pleased. She hugged Melia and said, 'Well, Miss Kind-Heart, if that isn't just like you!'

Two days later Grandpa arrived to take them all to the zoo. 'Now then,' he said, rattling the money in his pocket. 'Open up your moneyboxes, and I'll double all

you've got there! You must each pay all your own fares
and rides and tea, because I shall double your money.'

Jack had four shillings. Fanny had three shillings
and five pennies. The twins had two shillings and a
tuppence each.

'And what about Melia?' said Grandpa as he paid
out lots of money to the others.

'My box is empty,' said Melia, and she went red.
'I'm sorry, Grandpa. I'm no good at saving. Things
keep happening that make me spend my money. I'll
have to stay at home.'

'Oh, no you won't,' said Grandpa, and he took
Melia on his knee. 'Here's a little girl who can teach
all you others the right way to save and spend money!
She saved it up because she wanted to go to the zoo
as you all did – but when Benny was ill she made
him happy with a bunch of sweet peas bought out of
her money.

'And she gave her teacher all her savings for the old
woman who wanted new glasses. And then, when she

had saved up again Granny broke her leg, and Melia was the only one who thought Granny more important than her money, and spent every penny of it to cheer her up.'

Nobody said a word. They all suddenly felt rather mean. 'Melia,' said Grandpa, 'I'm proud of you! It's good to save money – but it's better to spend it the right way when you have to. You know how to save – and you know how to spend. I shall give you ten shillings for yourself to spend at the zoo. Come along.'

So off they all went – and how happy Melia was as she skipped along by her grandpa. He hadn't laughed at her. He hadn't scolded her. He had understood that she had to be kind and generous with her money as well as careful to save it up. Dear old Grandpa.

I think Melia was right, don't you? It's good to save, but it's even better to be kind when you see the chance.

It's a Rainy Day

It's a Rainy Day

'I'M SURE Aunt Twinkle will make us go and do all
the shopping for her today,' said Snip. 'She said if it
was fine, we'd have to go.'

'And it's as fine as can be,' said Snap, looking out of
the window.

'And we did want to finish making that aeroplane!'
said Snorum. 'Shopping is a perfect nuisance. I don't
want to go. Why doesn't it rain?'

'I say, you've given me an idea!' said Snip at once.
'Half a minute. I'll be back!'

He ran downstairs and out into the garden shed.
When he came back he was carrying two watering

cans. Snap and Snorum stared in surprise.

'Now listen,' said Snip. 'The kitchen window is just below our playroom, and Aunt Twinkle will be working there all morning. Suppose we fill a watering can and tip it out of our playroom window, what will Aunt Twinkle see down in the kitchen below, if she looks out of *her* window?'

'Rain!' said Snap and Snorum at once, and they roared with laughter. 'The water will sprinkle down out of the can, and she'll think it's raining. Hurray!'

'Yes,' said Snap, pleased. 'We can take it in turns to fill the first can and empty it, and while it's making rain for Aunt Twinkle to see, we'll be filling the second can, so that the rain never stops! One of us must go down and tell Aunt Twinkle it's raining so that we can't go shopping!'

Well, what a trick to think of! Just like those three mischievous imps!

Snip began to fill a can. Snap stood ready to take it to the window. Snorum ran down to the kitchen to his aunt.

'Ah, there you are, Snorum,' said Aunt Twinkle. 'I want you to go shopping for me, all three of you. There's a long list this morning.'

'You said we needn't go if it was raining,' said Snorum.

'Well, it isn't,' said his aunt.

And just at that very minute Snap took the watering can to the window upstairs, tipped it up and down came a great spatter of drops, looking for all the world like rain!

'There – look – it's started to *pour*,' said Snorum, trying not to giggle.

Aunt Twinkle looked up in astonishment. 'Well, I *am* surprised. It didn't look a bit like rain. Perhaps it will stop in a minute.'

But it didn't, of course, because upstairs Snip and Snap were hard at work filling the cans and emptying them out of the window. Soon the kitchen window below was running with drops, and Aunt Twinkle thought it must be really pouring!

'It looks as if it's set in for the morning,' she said. 'Very well, you needn't go shopping for me. I don't want you to get wet through. Go back upstairs and play with the others.'

Snorum was glad. Up he went, and told them the good news. 'We'll just empty a can out occasionally now,' he said. 'Just to keep the drops running down the kitchen window. Come on – let's get on with the aeroplane.'

Now, after about half an hour, someone came up the garden path. It was Mr Kindly, and Aunt Twinkle was very pleased to see him.

'I've just come to ask if you'll let Snip, Snap and Snorum come with me and have dinner in the town, and go to see a conjuring show afterwards,' said Mr Kindly. 'I've got the tickets.'

'But it's pouring with rain!' said Aunt Twinkle, looking at the drops running down the kitchen window.

'Oh, no, it's not,' said Mr Kindly in surprise. 'Look, I'm not a bit wet. It's fine and dry. I can't *think* why your window is so wet. A pipe must be leaking just above it.'

He went out to see and, of course, he saw the spout of the watering can sticking out of the playroom window above, and he guessed at once what the three imps were up to. They didn't want to go shopping!

'I suppose they don't like going shopping in the rain?' said Mr Kindly, coming back.

'No. They haven't got mackintoshes, so they get wet through,' said Aunt Twinkle. 'But I can't understand why you are so dry, Mr Kindly. It really *is* pouring down with rain!'

'It isn't,' said Mr Kindly, and he told her what he had seen. 'You've got three selfish, lazy little imps here, Mrs Twinkle. *I'm* not going to take them to dinner and to a conjuring show! I'll ask Pippin, Poppin and Skip next door instead.'

And with that out went Mr Kindly.

Aunt Twinkle called Snip, Snap and Snorum down to her. 'Mr Kindly just called in,' she said. 'He had tickets for a conjuring show this afternoon, and wanted to take you all to it, and out to dinner first. But I told him how you hated to go out in the rain – so he's gone next door to ask Pippin, Poppin and Skip. They'll *love* it!'

'Oh, don't let *them* go!' cried Snip. 'We'd love to go! Rain won't hurt us.'

'Oh, yes, it will,' said Aunt Twinkle firmly. 'If you can't go out into the rain to do my shopping, you can't possibly walk all the way to the next village. You'd be *soaked*!'

Snip, Snap and Snorum went back upstairs looking very gloomy indeed.

Aunt Twinkle called after them. 'And would you like to take those watering cans back to the shed? You won't need them any more now.'

What a shock they got! They did feel ashamed.

'We'd better go and say we're sorry,' said Snip when they had taken back the watering cans. 'We shan't get any cakes for tea if we don't!'

So they walked into the kitchen again.

'We're sorry, Aunt Twinkle,' said Snip. 'Very sorry. And we'll go and do your shopping this afternoon, we promise we will!'

Would you believe it, just before they set out, it began to *pour* with rain! It simply fell down in sheets. Real rain this time, not watering-can rain!

But Aunt Twinkle made them go shopping just the same. 'Promises must be kept, rain or no rain,' she said. 'It serves you right for being mean. Off you go, all of you, with my big umbrella between you.'

And there they go, very sorry for themselves indeed. Watering-can rain indeed! What a thing to do!

The Conceited Prince

The Conceited Prince

THERE ONCE lived a prince who was very rich. He had a wonderful palace, marvellous gardens and enough carriages and horses to last him for a lifetime.

Sometimes he would stand at the window and look out over his beautiful land. 'Ah!' he said. 'There is no other prince so rich as I am! And there is no other who has so many beautiful horses and dresses!'

Now, one day the king and queen of Fairyland wrote to say they were coming to visit him. This put the prince in a great flurry and fluster, for it was such a great honour to entertain the rulers of Fairyland!

So he began straight away to get things ready. He

decided he would meet the king and queen at the head of a great and grand procession. He would put on his beautiful feathered hat, his wonderful red shoes and his peacock-blue cloak. He would lead the procession, holding his handsome head well up, and stepping out grandly in his fine new shoes.

On the day when the king and queen were coming he dressed himself carefully. He was upset to find it was raining as he dressed, but he hoped that it was nothing but a shower. At last everything was ready, and when the prince stepped to the head of his grand procession the sun was shining.

Up the street he stepped haughtily, his feathers waving in the wind and his jewels gleaming. In the distance came the carriage of the king and queen.

The carriage drove up to the prince and the king leant out to greet him. The prince stepped grandly up to the carriage with his head well up in the air, and he didn't see that a large, shining rain puddle lay directly in front of him. Splash! In he went, and the water rose right over his new red shoes. He was so astonished that he lost his balance and fell, and – splish, splash! – there was the proud prince sitting in the middle of a muddy puddle!

'Ha, ha, ha!' laughed the king. 'Forgive me, prince, but it is the funniest thing I've seen for years! You looked funny enough stalking along in your fine feathers and shoes, but you're funnier still now!'

The prince rose to his feet, dripping with water and furiously angry. But he dared not show his anger, for he guessed he had displeased the king by his conceit.

But the queen was sorry for him.

'Never mind, prince,' she said. 'Perhaps you didn't know that *puddles lie in wait for the proud*! Cheer up. You'll be a happier prince now that you know.'

And she was quite right. He was.

The Umbrella Elf

The Umbrella Elf

THERE WAS an elf called Brollie, who sold the prettiest umbrellas you could wish to see. The fairy folk loved them.

Now one year came a winter that was very dry indeed, and nobody bought umbrellas. Brollie was upset, for he thought that he would soon be poor. So he thought of a very clever idea.

He went to the witch who lived in Sky Castle, and asked her for a hundred tiny rain clouds. She charged him a penny each for them, so he had to pay her a lot of money.

He showed his brother Binkie what he had bought,

and Binkie was very much astonished.

'What do you want silly things like that for?' he asked.

'Listen,' said Brollie. 'I want you to do something for me, Binkie. Do you see that very high tree just near my shop? Well, you're to climb up to the top with these little rain clouds, and wait there until someone comes by. Then you must let one of the clouds loose, so that it will shower down rain on the passerby. Then he will come into my shop and buy an umbrella!'

'That sounds very clever,' said Binkie. 'I'll do it!' So he climbed up the big tree with all the rain clouds, and waited till a fairy came by, dressed in her best. Binkie let loose a little cloud, and – pitter-patter! – the rain came pouring down on the fairy.

'Oh, dear!' she cried, and rushed into Brollie's shop to buy an umbrella.

The next day, and the next, the same thing happened, and soon Brollie's clouds were all used up, and he went to buy four hundred more. He had sold so many umbrellas that he was getting quite rich again.

But the next day who should come by but the Lord High Chamberlain, who had the very sharpest eyes in the kingdom. It had been a fine, warm day when he started out, without a cloud in the sky – but when he got near Brollie's shop it suddenly poured with rain!

'Strange!' said the chamberlain, and looked up into the sky – and what did he see peeping out of the big tree but Binkie, holding a lot of small rain clouds ready to set free when he wished to.

'Ho!' said the chamberlain. 'I see through this trick! Very clever and very naughty. Brollie! BROLLIE!'

Out came the elf, shivering and shaking, for he knew that his trick had been discovered.

'Take those clouds back to the witch,' ordered the chamberlain. 'Give me half the money you've earned in the last few days for the fairies' hospital, and promise to be good in the future!'

'I promise,' said Brollie, glad to be let off so lightly.

Poor Binkie! When he heard that the chamberlain

himself had been rained on he got such a fright that he fell right out of the tree. The clouds flew off by themselves, and where do you think they went to? To our land, and you'll probably see them there this April! Little clouds that bring rain for a minute or two, and then out shines the sun again, and we say, 'Why, that was an April shower!'

The Toy
Telephone

The Toy Telephone

JOHN HAD a toy telephone for his birthday. It was just like a real one, but the only thing wrong with it was that when John picked up the receiver and spoke into it nobody answered him.

So he had to speak for himself and for the person he was speaking to as well. Sometimes he rang up the dog next door and sometimes he rang up his friends and pretended to ask them to a party.

The telephone was green and had a place to speak into and a place to listen at. It stood on the table where John's farm was set out and looked very grand and grown-up.

One night a very strange thing happened. John was in bed, half asleep, when he heard the sound of little high voices in the nursery next to his bedroom. At first he thought he must be dreaming, then he knew he wasn't because he could hear the wind and the rain so clearly against the door.

'It surely can't be my *toys* that are talking together!' said John, feeling excited. 'No, it surely can't.'

He sat up in bed and listened. Yes, there was no doubt about it at all – there *were* people talking in the nursery and they had high birdlike voices, very sweet to listen to.

'I'm going to see who's there,' said John. He slipped on his dressing gown and crept to the door. He went to the nursery and peeped in to see who was there, expecting to see his toys playing about.

But the toys were all exactly as he had left them! Most of them were in the toy cupboard, his teddy was in the armchair and the farmyard was set out on the little table where the telephone stood.

John stared around the room. The fire was flickering and it wasn't difficult to see. And then John saw something rather surprising!

Sitting on the hearth rug, drying themselves, were four tiny creatures with wings. They were talking together in birdlike voices and John stared at them in the greatest surprise. At first he thought they were big moths, but soon he saw that they were pixies.

'Wow!' he said, going right into the room. 'I say! Who *are* you?'

The pixies sprang to their feet. But when they saw John's delighted face they smiled up at him.

'We are four pixies, caught out in the rain,' said one in a voice like a robin's, sweet and high. 'We flew in at the window to get dry. We *are* dry now – but we don't know whether to start out again or not, because if it goes on raining, we shall get soaked. And Twinky here has already sneezed three times.'

Twinky sneezed a fourth time and the other pixies looked at him anxiously.

'I suppose you aren't any good at telling the weather, are you?' asked Twinky.

John shook his head. 'No,' he said. 'I can never seem to tell if it is going to be fine or wet. If our grandpa were here, he could tell you, but he isn't. He always knows the weather.'

'Perhaps he knows the weather clerk,' said Twinky. 'The weather clerk lives up in the sky, you know, and always knows what weather is coming. I shouldn't be surprised if your grandpa is friends with him.'

'I don't think so,' said John, rather astonished. 'True, he always *does* look up at the sky when he tells me what the weather is going to be – but he has never said anything to me about the weather clerk!'

'I wish we could telephone to the weather clerk,' sighed Twinky. 'Then we should know what the weather will be for the rest of the night. We should know whether to stay here or whether to go on.'

John suddenly remembered his toy telephone. He reached it down from the table. 'Look!' he said.

'Here's a telephone! It's my own. You can use it if you like. But I must tell you that although it's easy to speak into, it is very, very difficult to hear anyone talking back to you.'

'Oh, we can easily get on to the weather clerk by using a little magic!' cried Twinky, sneezing again. He rubbed the telephone all over with his tiny handkerchief and then spoke into it.

'Hallo! Hallo! Is that the weather clerk? It is? Good! Then listen, weather clerk. This is Twinky the pixie speaking. It's just this minute stopped raining. Is it going to rain or blow any more tonight? If it isn't, we can set out again in safety and go home.'

John heard a tiny voice talking back down the telephone, but he couldn't hear what it said. Twinky heard, though, and nodded to the others. 'It's all right,' he said. 'We can go. There'll be no more rain tonight. Goodbye, John. And thank you so much for letting us use your telephone!'

Before John could say more than goodbye, the four

tiny creatures flew out of the window and were gone in the dark night. John looked at his telephone. He picked up the receiver and spoke softly into it.

'Are you still there, weather clerk? Is it going to be fine tomorrow? I want to have a picnic.'

A tiny voice answered him from far away. 'Yes, it will be fine tomorrow. You can have your picnic.'

'Oh, thank you!' said John joyfully, and crept back to bed. Sure enough, the weather clerk was right, and it *was* fine all the next day. And, do you know, John *always* knows exactly what the weather is going to be, and I can guess why. It's because he can speak to the weather clerk on his toy telephone whenever he wants to. Dear me, don't I wish he would lend it to me just for two minutes!

The Lost Doll's Pram

The Lost Doll's Pram

'MUMMY, I do so wish Tibbles wouldn't keep jumping into my doll's pram,' said Ellie. 'How can I stop her?'

'Well, you could stop her by doing what I used to do when you were a baby in your pram,' said her mother. 'You can put a net over the pram so that no cat can jump into it.'

'Oh, dear, I don't want to do that,' said Ellie. 'It would be an awful bother to have to do that every time I put my dolls to sleep. I shall shout at Tibbles next time I find her in my doll's pram!'

Ellie found her there the very next morning, curled up under the eiderdown, fast asleep. Didn't Ellie shout! Tibbles gave a miaow of surprise, and leapt out at once. She was never shouted at by Ellie and she didn't like it at all.

'You are *not* to get into the pram,' said Ellie to Tibbles. 'I have told you ever so often. You are a naughty little cat. Do you want to smother Rosebud or Josephine by lying on top of them? Shoo! Go away!'

Tibbles ran away – but will you believe it, as soon as Ellie went indoors again, Tibbles jumped right into the pram once more!

She did love that pram. It was so soft inside and so cosy. She loved cuddling down, curling herself up and going to sleep in peace and quiet there.

It just fits me nicely, she thought. *I can share it with the dolls. They never seem to mind. They don't even kick me.*

Now the next day three naughty boys came along with a naughty little girl. They saw some apples hanging on the trees in Ellie's garden, and they crept in at the gate to take some.

Ellie saw them from the window. She rushed out

into the garden. 'You bad children! That's stealing! Go away and leave my daddy's apples alone.'

'Give us some!' shouted the biggest boy.

'No, certainly not. If you had come to ask my daddy properly, he would have given you a basketful,' cried Ellie. 'But people who steal don't get any. Go away!'

'You're a horrid little girl!' shouted the boy. 'We'll pay you back!'

And then Ellie's mother came out and the four naughty children ran away. They came peeping over the wall again the day after – but not to take the apples. They meant to pay Ellie back for sending them away.

'Look, there's her doll's pram,' whispered the little girl. 'Let's take it away into the park and hide it where she can't find it. That will teach her to shout at us and send us away. Quick, Billy – there's no one about – you slip in and get it.'

Billy opened the back gate, ran into the garden and took hold of the pram handle. He wheeled the little pram at top speed out of the gate. Slam! The gate shut and the four children hurried down the lane to the park.

'She hasn't got any dolls in the pram,' said the little girl. 'I'd have thrown them into the bushes if she had!'

What a very horrid little girl she was! She had dolls of her own and loved them – and yet she would have done an unkind thing to someone else's dolls! Well, well, some people are strange, aren't they?

The boys stuffed the pram into the middle of a big bush and left it there. Then they went back to Ellie's garden to see what she said when she came out and found her pram missing.

She soon came out with her two dolls, meaning to take them for a walk, as she always did each morning. But where was her pram? It was nowhere to be seen! Ellie looked everywhere for it and then she saw the four heads of the giggling children, peeping over the wall.

'Have you seen my pram?' she called.

'Yes,' they called back.

'Where is it?' shouted Ellie.

'It's hidden in the park where you can't find it!' called the biggest boy. 'Ha, ha! You'll never find it again!'

'Mummy, Mummy, come here!' called Ellie, almost in tears. But her mother had just gone next door and she didn't come. So Ellie had to make up her mind herself what she was going to do.

I must go and look in the park, she thought. *Oh, dear – suppose it rains? My lovely pram will be soaked. Suppose I don't find it? How am I to know where those bad children have put it?*

She put her dolls down just inside the house, ran down the garden again, into the lane, and was soon in the park. Now where should she look?

She hunted here and she hunted there. She looked in this bush and that, but she couldn't find her pram.

Oh, dear, there are such a lot of bushes and trees!

thought poor Ellie. *I could look all day long and never find my pram. Where can it be?*

It was very well hidden indeed. Someone else was well hidden there too. And that was Tibbles!

Tibbles had been in the pram when the bad children had run off with it, curled up as usual under the eiderdown, fast asleep. When the children had taken the pram Tibbles had thought it was Ellie taking the dolls for a walk. She hadn't dared to pop her head up in case Ellie was cross with her. So she just lay there, wondering why the pram went so fast that morning. Then suddenly it was pushed into the bushes, and was still. Tibbles shut her eyes and went to sleep again.

She woke up after a time and stretched herself. Everything seemed very quiet. Tibbles felt hungry and thought she would jump out of the pram and go and find her dinner. She had forgotten that the pram had been taken for a walk – she thought she was still in garden!

She poked her head out from under the covers and

looked around. What was this? She was somewhere quite strange! This wasn't her garden. Tibbles sat right up, very frightened.

Where was she? Where was Ellie? What had happened? And dear me, was this rain beginning to fall?

It was. Big drops pattered down on Tibbles, and she crouched down. She hated the rain. She suddenly felt very lonely and frightened and she gave a loud miaow.

'MEEOW! MEE-OW-EE-OW-EE-OW-EE-OW!'

Nothing happened except that the rain pattered down more loudly. One enormous drop fell – splash! – on to Tibbles's nose, and she miaowed angrily.

The rain made a loud noise on the bracken around, and Tibbles couldn't think what it was. She didn't dare to jump out of the pram.

'MEEOW-OW-OW!' she wailed at the top of her voice.

Ellie was not very far off, and she heard this last 'MEEOW'. She stopped. That sounded like a cat's voice! Was there a cat lost in the park, caught in the rain that was now pouring down? Poor thing!

'MEEEEEEEEE-OOOW-OOOOW!' wailed Tibbles, and Ellie hurried towards the sound. 'MEEE-OW!'

It seems to come from that bush over there, thought the little girl, and went to it. Another loud wail came from the spot.

'Meee-ow-ow-ow! MEE-ow-ow-OW!'

And then Ellie suddenly saw the handle of her pram sticking out of the bush. How delighted she was! She ran to it and gave the handle a tug – out came her doll's pram – and there, sitting in the middle of it, scared and lonely, was Tibbles! 'Oh, Tibbles! It was you I heard miaowing!' cried Ellie in surprise. 'You must have been asleep in the pram again when those children ran off with it. Oh, Tibbles, I am glad you were in it – it was your miaowing that made me find it! I'll never scold you again for getting into the pram!'

She put up the hood and drew the waterproof cover over Tibbles so that the frightened cat wouldn't get soaked. And then off she went home with her precious pram, not minding the rain in the least because she was so pleased to have found her pram again.

Tibbles couldn't imagine why Ellie made such a fuss of her, but she liked it all the same. The funny thing was that she never, never got into the doll's pram again. She was so afraid it would run off with her into the park and lose her!

So do you know what she does? She gets into the doll's cot up in the playroom and goes to sleep there! I've seen her, and she really does look sweet, curled up with her tail round her nose.

Frog Rain

Frog Rain

ONE MORNING in early spring all the ponds were full of excited, croaking frogs. They swam about happily in the warm sun. They laid thousands of eggs that swelled up and rose to the surface like lumps of white jelly speckled with black.

The black specks were the eggs, of course, and these hatched out into wriggling tadpoles. The pond was black with them! The fish gobbled up a good many. The black water beetle ate dozens for his meals every day. The big dragonfly grub, who lurked at the bottom of the pond, lay in wait for an unwary wriggler, caught him and ate him before he even knew what was happening!

But still there were hundreds and hundreds of tadpoles in the pond, growing bigger every day. They grew their back legs, and looked very comical. Then they grew their front legs, and began to look like tiny frogs. Their long tails gradually became shorter and shorter, and then one day when a large father frog hopped to the bank of the pond to have a swim he saw that there were no tadpoles there at all – but only hundreds and hundreds of restless baby frogs!

They swam in the pond. They stuck their blunt noses out of the water. They climbed up on the floating log in the pond and sat there, basking in the sun. They ate the tiny water insects for their dinner, and had a lovely time.

'You will have to leave the pond soon,' croaked the frog. 'It will be too crowded, and you will not have enough to eat. You must do as we big frogs have done – leave the water and find new homes for yourselves! There are cool ditches, where the flies hover. There are marshy meadows, damp and full of marsh flies to eat. There are green woodlands where little streams trickle.'

The tiny frogs listened and were eager to find new homes. 'Not yet, not yet,' warned the big frog. 'The weather is hot and dry. You will die if you try to travel in the scorched fields and dusty wayside. Wait till it rains hard – wait till the air is cool and wet. Then you can travel in comfort, with the rain on your back, and moisture under your feet!'

So the little frogs waited patiently through the hot summer days. And then there came a rainstorm. Oh, what a rainstorm it was! The rain poured down from the sky as if a giant watering can was being tilted over the earth. The drops fell down into the pond and made little rings all over it.

'It is time to travel!' croaked the little frogs. 'Come quickly!' And with one accord they all clambered out of the pond and set off in the rain to find new homes. They hopped in hundreds over the road, they crawled in crowds down the lanes, they settled in ditches and meadows – they were everywhere!

And people passing by exclaimed in surprise and said, 'Look at all these tiny frogs! They have come with the rain! It has been raining frogs! Let us write to the papers about it!'

And then, children, they wrote to the papers, and some of them solemnly printed a piece all about the curious frog rain. How all the little frogs croaked with laughter when they heard! 'The rain didn't bring us; we brought ourselves!' they said.

Have *you* ever read about frog rain in the papers?

Bessie's Butterfly

Bessie's Butterfly

BESSIE HAD a cold. She had been away from school for three days, but Mother said she could go back the next day. So Bessie was very pleased, because she loved school.

'It's nature lesson tomorrow,' she said. 'Good! I love nature lesson. Miss Brown has asked us to see what we can bring for the nature table tomorrow, Mother. I wonder what I can bring. Can I go out and see if I can find something this afternoon?'

'Yes, if it's fine,' said Mother. 'Maybe you will be able to find a little yellow coltsfoot, or perhaps a snowdrop in the garden, or a very early crocus or primrose. Or maybe you can pick some black ivy berries. They are ripe now, and the birds are eating them.'

'Oh, yes, there are lots of things to find,' said Bessie. 'I shall have my name on the nature chart, if I bring something that no one else has found. Billy had his name written on the chart last week because he brought a ladybird! Fancy that, Mother. You wouldn't think anybody could find a ladybird so early in the year, would you?'

'No, I wouldn't,' said Mother.

The afternoon came at last – and, oh, dear, what a pity, it was pouring with rain! Bessie looked out of the window and then went to Mother.

'It's raining,' she said, 'but I can put on my sou'wester and mackintosh, can't I?'

'No, Bessie, I'm afraid you can't,' said Mother. 'You might make your cold come back if you get wet again. You must play indoors.'

'Oh, Mother! But I shan't find anything for the

nature table then,' cried Bessie sadly. 'It's too bad. I did so want to.'

'Darling, I'm sorry,' said Mother. 'But I simply can't let you get wet. I don't want you to have to go to bed again. Now cheer up – go and play in the attic, if you like. It is warm up there, because the hot-water tank is there, and you will be as warm as toast.'

Bessie liked playing in the attic. It had two funny little windows, a big pile of old trunks, a huge shelf of old picture books and the tiny cot Bessie had had when she was a baby. It was fun to get into that and curl up and pretend she was tiny again.

But, oh, dear, what a pity she wouldn't be able to find anything to take to Miss Brown next day! Well, it couldn't be helped. Bessie wasn't going to sulk and grumble. She knew Mother hated that.

So up the stairs she went and into the attic. It looked very dusty. Bessie thought it would be fun to put on an apron and cap, and pretend to be Jane the maid, cleaning hard. So downstairs she went again, found an apron and made herself a cap out of a handkerchief. She borrowed a duster and a broom from Jane, and went up to do some cleaning.

And do you know what she found in a corner of the attic ceiling? A butterfly! Would you think anyone would find a butterfly so early in the year? Bessie couldn't believe her eyes! She had just been going to brush the cobwebs from the ceiling when she had seen the butterfly!

She looked at it – it seemed to be asleep. She touched it. It fluttered its wings softly. So it was alive!

Bessie took it gently into her hand and went down to Mother with it. 'Guess what I've got!' she said. And she opened her hand and showed Mother the butterfly.

'A peacock butterfly!' cried Mother in surprise. 'It must have been sleeping the cold days away, up in our attic, Bessie. They sometimes do that. How surprised Miss Brown will be to see a butterfly – that is far better than a ladybird!'

'I shall put it gently into a box with some holes in,'

said Bessie, pleased. 'And tomorrow I'll take it to school. I'm sure I shall have my name on the nature chart now! Oh, I am so pleased! What a good thing it poured with rain and I couldn't go out! I wouldn't have found the butterfly then.'

'And what a good thing you were nice about not going out, and went to cheerfully play in the attic!' said Mother. 'Well, you deserve your butterfly, Bessie!'

Bessie's name is on the nature chart! You can't think how proud she is to see it there!

Acknowledgements

All efforts have been made to seek necessary permissions.

The stories in this publication first appeared in the following publications:

'Mrs Twiddle's Umbrella' first appeared in *Enid Blyton's Sunny Stories*, No. 476, 1950.

'It's Going to Rain!' first appeared in *Enid Blyton's Sunny Stories*, No. 409, 1947.

'The Tale of Chuckle and Pip' first appeared in *Enid Blyton's Sunny Stories*, No. 127, 1939.

'The Little Sugar Mouse' first appeared as 'The Little Sugar-Mouse' in *Enid Blyton's Sunny Stories*, No. 256, 1941.

'Mr Binkle's Boots' first appeared as 'Mister Binkle's Boots' in *Sunny Stories for Little Folks*, No. 155, 1932.

'The Tale of Scissors the Gnome' first appeared in *The Teachers World*, No. 1840, 1938.

'This is My Place!' first appeared in *The Enid Blyton Nature Readers*, No. 33, published by Macmillan in 1955.

'Pixie Mirrors' first appeared in *Enid Blyton's Sunny Stories*, No. 228, 1941.

'Muddlesome's Mistake' first appeared in *Sunny Stories for Little Folks*, No. 74, 1929.

'Sally's Umbrella' first appeared in *The Bed That Ran Away and Other Stories*, published by Award in 2000.

'Mr Stamp-About Goes Shopping' first appeared in *Enid Blyton's Magazine*, No. 6, Vol. 5, 1957.

'Pinkity's Pranks' first appeared as 'The Pranks of Pinkity' in *Leicester Advertiser*, No. 4941, 1923.

'Rain in Toytown' first appeared in *Sunny Stories for Little Folks*, No. 250, 1936.

'A Tale of Shuffle, Trot and Merry' first appeared in *Enid Blyton's Magazine*, No. 10, Vol. 4, 1956.

'Mr Big-Hat's Button' first appeared in *Enid Blyton's Sunny Stories*, No. 393, 1946.

'Umbrella Weather' first appeared in *The Enid Blyton Nature Readers*, No. 32, published by Macmillan in 1955.

'Mr Meddle's Umbrella' first appeared as 'Mister Meddle's Umbrella' in *Enid Blyton's Sunny Stories*, No. 246, 1941.

'The Secret Door' first appeared in *Enid Blyton's Sunny Stories*, No. 411, 1947.

'The Blow-Abouts' first appeared in *Sunny Stories for Little Folks*, No. 69, 1929.

'Melia's Moneybox' first appeared as 'Melia's Money Box' in *The Enid Blyton Pennant Readers*, No. 1, 1950.

'It's a Rainy Day' first appeared as 'It's Pouring with Rain!' in *Enid Blyton's Sunny Stories*, No. 537, 1952.

'The Conceited Prince' first appeared in *The Teachers World*, No. 999, 1923.

'The Umbrella Elf' first appeared in *The Teachers World*, No. 1401, 1930.

'The Toy Telephone' first appeared in *Enid Blyton's Sunny Stories*, No. 238, 1941.

'The Lost Doll's Pram' first appeared in *Enid Blyton's Sunny Stories*, No. 531, 1952.

'Frog Rain' first appeared as 'Frog-Rain' in *The Teachers World*, No. 1884, 1939.

'Bessie's Butterfly' first appeared in *Enid Blyton's Sunny Stories*, No. 158, 1940.

Enid Blyton

NATURE STORIES

30 stories

*Explore the great outdoors with
these short stories by the
world's best-loved storyteller!*

Enid Blyton

is one of the most popular children's authors of all time. Her books have sold over 500 million copies and have been translated into other languages more often than any other children's author.

Enid Blyton adored writing for children. She wrote over 700 books and about 2,000 short stories. *The Famous Five* books, now 75 years old, are her most popular. She is also the author of other favourites including *The Secret Seven*, *The Magic Faraway Tree*, *Malory Towers* and *Noddy*.

Born in London in 1897, Enid lived much of her life in Buckinghamshire and loved dogs, gardening and the countryside. She was very knowledgeable about trees, flowers, birds and animals.

Dorset – where some of the Famous Five's adventures are set – was a favourite place of hers too.

Enid Blyton's stories are read and loved by millions of children (and grown-ups) all over the world. Visit enidblyton.co.uk to discover more.